SILENCE

Michael Innes is the pseudonym of J. I. M. Stewart. Educated at Edinburgh Academy and Oriel College, Oxford, he has been Student of Christ Church, Oxford, and Reader in English Literature at the University of Oxford. He has published many novels under his own name – including the quintet *A Staircase in Surrey* – and several volumes of short stories and essays. As Michael Innes, Dr Stewart combined a polished literary wit with a classical whodunit, and is generally credited with the appearance of the donnish detective story. He has written a prodigious number of crime novels including *Death at the President's Lodging*, *Hamlet, Revenge!*, *Lament for a Maker* and *Appleby's End*. He lives in Yorkshire.

SILENCE OBSERVED

by

Michael Innes

GOLLANCZ CRIME

Gollancz Crime is an imprint of Victor Gollancz Ltd
14 Henrietta Street, London WC2E 8QJ

First published in Great Britain 1961
by Victor Gollancz Ltd

First Gollancz Crime edition 1992

A catalogue record for this book is available
from the British Library

ISBN 0 575 05381 X

Printed and bound in Great Britain
by Cox & Wyman Ltd, Reading

CHAPTER ONE

"I'VE GOT SOMETHING uncommonly interesting here," Charles Gribble said.

Gribble, with a small bundle of papers in his hand, was standing directly in front of the fireplace. Just above his head, therefore, hung a notice which read:

SILENCE IS OBSERVED.

The committee was rather fond of notices. Some members said that the club was plastered with them in a thoroughly irritating way. They were couched in various grammatical forms, with perhaps a preponderant inclination towards passive or impersonal constructions. *It is earnestly desired by the committee* . . . was a favourite opening. The only tabu seemed to be on positive commands and injunctions. Hence the simple statement: *Silence is observed*.

"Something really uncommonly interesting," Gribble said in a rather louder voice.

There were only two other men in the room. One was Sir John Appleby. The other, unidentifiable behind a newspaper, was clearly a man of resource. For, as Gribble spoke for the second time, the newspaper sank gently down upon its owner's face and stomach, and from beneath it came the first of a regular succession of gentle snores.

"That so?" Appleby said half-heartedly, and put

down his coffee-cup. It was time he was getting back to his desk at Scotland Yard.

"And quite up your street, in a way," Gribble continued. "Just listen to this."

Appleby's heart sank. It was extraordinary what many people judged to be quite up the street of an elderly man absorbed in the administration of the Metropolitan Police. But he couldn't positively refuse to listen to Gribble, who wasn't a bad sort. He was a contemporary of Appleby's, and understood to hold some position of modest hereditary power in the City. Whether because of this or otherwise, he clearly owned considerable wealth—quite enough to indulge in the various literary and dilettante pursuits which were what drew him to this particular club. He came in almost every day and talked Christie's or Sotheby's with cronies. With Appleby he had a common interest in mediaeval English pottery, which had been a reasonable poor man's field thirty years ago. It wasn't that now. But Appleby still picked up a piece from time to time—and occasionally after consultation with Charles Gribble. It obviously wasn't pottery that Gribble had in his head now. But it was only civil to listen to him, all the same.

And Gribble glanced, not at the sheaf of papers he was holding, but at the ceiling of the little reading-room. It was rather as if he was about to make a speech.

"Many swarms of wild bees," Gribble said, "descended on our fields."

For a moment Appleby didn't make much of this. Then he understood.

"Is this to be a poem?" he asked.

Gribble nodded a shade impatiently.

"Of course it's a poem," he said. "It scans, doesn't it? I'll begin again.

> "*Many swarms of wild bees descended on our fields:*
>   *Stately stood the wheatstalk with head bent high:*
>   *Big of heart we labour'd at storing mighty yields,*
>   *Wool and corn, and clusters to make men cry!*"

Gribble took his glance from the ceiling and looked at Appleby. "What do you remember about that?" he asked.

Appleby shook his head—with the odd result that something floated into it.

"God!" Appleby said.

Gribble beamed.

"That's it, my dear fellow. You're right on the spot. Just go ahead."

And, with another second for thought, Appleby went ahead:

> "*God! of whom music*
>   *And song and blood are pure,*
>   *The day is never darken'd*
>   *That had thee here obscure.*"

He glanced at Gribble. "That right? Meredith, isn't it?"

"Precisely, Appleby, precisely! George Meredith's 'Phoebus with Admetus'. Every stanza ends with the four short lines that you've quoted. Rather a lovely effect, to my mind. There's great charm in a really cunningly contrived refrain."

"No doubt," Appleby said. "But I don't quite see——"

"And *now* listen!" This time, Gribble applied himself, not to the ceiling, but to his papers:

> *"Purple glowed the clusters ripened on our vines,*
> *Golden was our honey in the cool dark combs,*
> *Golden gleamed the metal wrested from our mines,*
> *Purple were the hangings in our high proud homes."*

Gribble paused from his reading and looked up. He was evidently in a mood of modest triumph.

"Do you remember *that*?" he asked.

"I can't say that I do." Appleby frowned. "And I have a very fair memory for verse, as it happens—although declaiming it isn't much in my line. And I'm blessed if I recall that bit about our vines and mines and combs and homes. Or all that about purple and gold. Not quite up to the rest of the poem, is it?"

"Um," Gribble said. He didn't look too pleased.

"'High proud homes', was it?" Appleby went on. He felt like mildly teasing Gribble. "Of course Meredith could be terribly vulgar. But homes like that sound to me a bit too much like Gracious Living and all that—even for Meredith."

Gribble chuckled. Or rather, it wasn't quite a chuckle, which is essentially a plebeian sort of thing. The sound emitted by Charles Gribble was conditioned by the existence of three or four generations of Gribbles flourishing on banking or whatever. And it seemed to hold a suggestion of—so to speak—wheels quite enchantingly within wheels. There was, it appeared, some quite enormous joke that Appleby wasn't yet within a mile of.

"Well, yes," Gribble said. "Meredith could strike

uncertain notes. And perhaps 'high proud homes' would be one—eh?" Gribble momentarily put down his papers in order to rub his hands together. "Meredith never quite got clear of his grandfather's tailor's shop. But he tried. He tried damned hard. Perhaps that's what he's doing here. Would that be it, Appleby? I mean to say, that's how your mind would work, isn't it, if I told you that Meredith had scrapped this 'proud homes' stanza? Struck it out, you know, before the poem was published. That would be why you don't remember these particular lines. Eh—my dear Appleby? Lines existing"—Gribble was clutching his papers again, and now he flourished them—"only in manuscript."

"Now I understand you." Appleby had no difficulty in showing decent interest. "You've secured a batch of Meredith's manuscripts?"

Gribble again produced his gilt-edged chuckle.

"That's the inference," he said. "That's the inference, certainly. Holograph, you know. Are you acquainted with Meredith's fist? Highly idiosyncratic. Spot it anywhere."

"Most satisfactory," Appleby said—having glanced at the sheet thrust at him. And he could understand Gribble's sense of triumph. His bundle of papers was a substantial one. He must have come by this unpublished material of Meredith's in quite a big way, and he was losing no time in crowing over it.

Probably, too, Gribble had paid a great deal for the stuff. The market for such things was now entirely mad. And soon Gribble would no doubt publish his find, with appropriate critical remarks, on the back page of *The Times Literary Supplement.* Which was very harmless—very harmless, indeed. Appleby wondered why it was supposed to be up his street.

"Most satisfactory," he repeated cordially. "You've really got hold of quite a lot of unpublished material by Meredith?"

"My dear chap, it's not *by* Meredith!" Gribble produced a laugh which, although exuberant, still seemed to ring decorously of the most respectable propertied classes. "It's much better fun than if it were *by* Meredith. And—oddly enough—I imagine it's worth much more, too."

And Gribble flourished his papers more unrestrainedly than before.

"Forgery, my dear boy," he said. "Forgery—every sheet of it!"

"Well—that does sound a little up my street, I agree." Appleby felt that, as a policeman, he could say no less than this. "But do I understand that you're proposing to invoke the aid of the law? People commonly do, when they've been swindled. And yet you don't *look* as if you were feeling particularly indignant about it all."

"Swindled!" Now Gribble *was* indignant. "*Me* swindled? I assure you, Appleby, such a thing has never happened to me in my life. These papers are forgery, and as forgery I've acquired them. And I assure you that the job is absolutely first-class of its kind."

"It all purports to be rejected passages and early drafts and so on?"

Gribble nodded.

"Most of it does. And there's a very clever idea at the bottom of it, you'll agree. Take the bits of 'Phoebus with Admetus' we've been considering. 'Many swarms of wild bees'—you remember? That's the authentic Meredith, and first class. Then 'Purple glowed the clusters' and so on. That's the forgery I've got here." And Gribble tapped his papers. "You—having, if I may say so, a developed taste in poetry, my dear Appleby— felt it at once to be rather inferior. But that, of course, is just what we'd expect, even supposing the stanza really to be Meredith's. *He* thought it inferior—and therefore he rejected it. The supposed situation allows the forger a little margin, so to speak. He need never be quite as good as the poet himself."

"Clever," Appleby said. "Yes, I agree it's clever. But a forger who is also an artist——"

Gribble beamed.

"Exactly! He will really want to equal his original now and then. And this stuff"—again Gribble tapped the papers—"does include a couple of efforts that aren't meant to be thought of as belonging to the rejected order. There's a complete companion poem to 'Love in the Valley'—which is possibly Meredith's most famous thing—and an entire additional section to 'The Woods of Westermain' which would absolutely defy detection. But then, we're dealing with Manallace, you know. This Meredith stuff is by Manallace himself. Perhaps you didn't know that I'm forming a collection of work by the really great forgers? Manallace comes right at the top."

"So I understand." Appleby thought he sounded

suitably impressed. Manallace—the younger Manallace—had been a very famous literary forger indeed.

"There isn't the slightest question about it." Gribble spoke as weightily as if he were laying down vital policy to a board of directors. "Mind you, the elder Manallace's Chaucer forgery was pretty good. But it was young Geoffrey Manallace who had *range*. Quite first-class on typography, and quite first-class on manuscript material as well. And yet, although he *had* range, he didn't over-produce. That's the final charm of Geoffrey Manallace."

"I see," Appleby said. "Scarcity value."

"Yes, indeed. And a good deal that he *did* produce, he didn't *market*. Of course he had no economic motive to do so—or none worth speaking of. He was a wealthy man, and what prompted him to his forgeries was vanity and a perverted sense of fun. But apparently he developed compunctions. I haven't got the whole story. But it seems there was a woman in it."

"Ah," Appleby said. This seemed the appropriate comment here.

"Yes, it seems there was a woman who pulled him up—so far as making money out of his queer talent was concerned."

"Edifying," Appleby said. "Geoffrey Manallace was reclaimed by the love of a pure woman. But, of course, that may be a forgery too. He may well have left hints for a bogus life-story, as well as plenty of bogus Meredith."

"That's no doubt true. But, whatever the actual truth of the matter, it's certain that Manallace kept a considerable amount of really superb forgery tucked away in a drawer. And this Meredith effort I've been lucky enough to come by is the absolute gem of the whole thing. There are several other keen collectors of forgeries, you know, including a couple of Americans to whom money means nothing at all. But with *these*"— and this time Gribble positively stroked his papers— "I think I may say I'm a good step ahead."

"I congratulate you," Appleby said. "And the stuff really has the curious interest of being technically impeccable and undetectable? There are so many scientific tests nowadays."

"Very true, my dear fellow. Photography under all those deuced cunning rays, and that sort of thing. But Geoffrey Manallace was years ahead of his time. He thought of everything. For instance, I've been at the ink. This forged 'Phoebus with Admetus' stanza turns out to be written in ink that went out of production in 1907. One wonders how he came by that. It's an example of the perfect detail. Meredith, you'll remember, died in 1909."

"If he was a good enough chemist," Appleby said, "Manallace could probably analyse old ink on a page, and then make up an ink which was chemically indistinguishable from it."

"Quite so. To be a really good forger or faker nowadays a fellow has to be both an artist and a scientist. A perfect Leonardo, in fact. That's no doubt part of the fascination of it. Take the manufacture of paper. Materials and processes are always changing, and an eye has to be kept on that. And there's some nice old paper here. I've been having a look at it."

As he said this, Gribble moved away from the empty

fireplace before which he had been absent-mindedly thinking to warm himself and walked over to a window. There he held up the first sheet between himself and the view of Pall Mall.

"Yes," he said. "Yes, indeed." And he held up the second sheet. There was a silence—rather a long silence, broken only by the resolute snores of the man beneath the newspaper.

"Well?" Appleby said.

But—very evidently—it wasn't well. Gribble was standing frozen and like a man transformed. When he spoke, it was in a new and troubled voice.

"Appleby—come over here. But I must be wrong, of course. I'll be forgetting the date of my own birth next." He gave a shaky laugh. "For God's sake—come *here*!"

Appleby crossed the room. Gribble's index-finger, trembling with agitation, was resting on the bottom left-hand corner of the sheet. Against the clear sunlight it was possible to distinguish a complicated little arabesque of lighter tone.

"I suppose you know your watermarks?" Gribble asked huskily.

"Good Lord, no!" Appleby laughed. "It's something I remember having to get up once or twice, long ago. But I've clean forgotten all that technical stuff, I'm ashamed to say. At the Yard I've got a young man who knows the rudiments of paper—chemical processes, watermarks and all. And I'd go to a fellow in the British Museum, if I wanted more."

"You could come to *me*, for that matter. For I *do* know. And it's no use pretending. I'm just *not* making a mistake now. *This* watermark"—and Gribble tapped the paper—"first appeared in 1924. Look—it's on only one of the sheets of this Meredith stuff. And, indeed, there's only about a third of it on that. But it's fatal to the whole damned thing."

Appleby couldn't help laughing. He could remember plenty of occasions on which little snags of this sort had meant the difference between guilt and innocence in grave matters. So Gribble's seemed to him to be a very absurd and comical sort of dismay.

"Too bad," he said. "The great Geoffrey Manallace slipping up for once. But never mind. Perhaps it gives his Meredith forgery a bigger scarcity value than ever. It may represent the unique occasion on which Manallace *did* slip up."

But at this—very strangely—Gribble gave what could only be described as a howl of rage. It was so alarming a demonstration that Appleby could hear, behind him, the supposedly slumbering man jump up and hasten from the room.

"You bloody fool!" Gribble cried—and it would have been impossible to tell whether he was addressing Appleby or apostrophizing himself. "Geoffrey Manallace—don't you *know*, God help you?—Geoffrey Manallace died in 1922."

Appleby—although not precisely slow-witted even in what he had come to think of as his declining years—took a second to get at this. When he did, he once more couldn't help laughing.

"I congratulate you again," he said presently. "Here is a completely new category of rarities. You and your fellow collectors have bumped up the value of Manallace's forgeries to the point at which it becomes worth some ingenious person's while to forge some. A forged forgery! I declare, I've never heard of such a thing before. Positively, my dear Gribble, it ought to be the pride of your collection."

But Charles Gribble refused to see the joke. Appleby was confirmed in the view that he had paid quite a lot of money for what he'd thought was Manallace's Meredith. And its turning out to be—as one might say—X's Manallace's Meredith was upsetting him correspondingly.

Still, the money couldn't mean much to Gribble. It was his vanity—his specialized collector's vanity—and not his pocket that had received the really severe blow. Hadn't he been declaring, rather noisily, that he'd never been swindled in his life? Well, now he had been. And—what was worse—he'd slipped up in a humiliatingly elementary way. Not to have scanned every inch of those papers for watermarks before putting down his cheque was a beginner's error in this particular game.

"Well, well," Appleby said comfortingly, "I suppose you can take the matter up with your dealer, whoever he was. If you're an important customer of his, he won't be disposed to stand by the principle of *caveat emptor*. He'll cancel the deal—and keep quiet about it, too."

Gribble was now looking puzzled as well as angry.

"That's no doubt true," he said. "He's a little fellow with whom I've done a good many deals. And entirely reliable in what he tells you about the provenance and so forth of what you buy."

"But he doesn't always tell you a great deal?"

"Oh, exactly. These fellows often have to be very discreet. And that makes it correspondingly important that one should be able to trust their word absolutely. Otherwise one may find oneself embarrassingly mixed up in questions of legal title and so on. This little chap has a high reputation. And when he explained to me that there had been a lady involved—a lady very decidedly in Geoffrey Manallace's confidence who was equally decidedly not Geoffrey Manallace's wife—I was perfectly willing to leave it at that. But now I must take it up with him. I'm confident he hasn't been consciously cheating me. It's he who's been had."

"At least in the first instance," Appleby said. "But, even if you've been had too, mayn't you be on to something rather interesting? This forger of forgeries may operate in quite a big way—and he's clearly up to the standards of Manallace himself. Moreover, you are at this moment the only person to have tumbled to his existence. Go after him. Study the finer points of his technique—and then look around for more of him in the light of that knowledge. You might manage a virtual corner in him. The situation, to my mind, is full of promise."

Gribble brightened. If he recognised irony in this, he didn't resent it.

"Perhaps there's something in what you say," he admitted. "Yes, there's something in it." He looked more cheerfully at his sheaf of papers, and then thrust them into a pocket. "And I'll start by having a word with my little chap. Share a cab? Bloomsbury's my direction."

Appleby shook his head, and watched Gribble out of the room. Gribble, it occurred to him, had shown the true collector's instinctive caginess in failing to mention the little chap's name. And Appleby glanced at the notice above the chimney-piece. It fitted, he thought. That sort of acquisitive world is one in which, habitually, a good deal of

SILENCE IS OBSERVED.

CHAPTER TWO

Simple persons, of unassuming colloquial speech, will sometimes be heard to remark that one damned thing leads to another. But policemen are only too happy when it does. A distinguishable sequence or concatenation between events is just what they are after. And when one thing merely *follows* another they are sometimes a little slow to see that it is anything more than that. Appleby was going to feel that he had been slow in just this way in what he thought of at first as the Manallace affair.

He had dropped into his club again at six. It was something he did twice a week for the purpose of glancing through a few continental newspapers. And this, of course, took him back to the little reading-room.

He settled in with that morning's *Figaro*.

"Come out of this morgue," a voice murmured. "We'll have a drink."

A bishop who was reading the *New Yorker* looked round disapprovingly, pointed a solemn episcopal finger at the notice over the chimney-piece, and then returned to his studies.

It was an elderly man with a short grey beard who had paused for a moment beside Appleby's chair. Sir Gabriel Gulliver was the Director of an august national institution. He was also some sort of connection of Appleby's wife. So Appleby rose and followed him from the slumberous room. They walked in silence

down the great staircase and into the hall. Through
tall glass doors London showed rain-sodden and
cheerless.

"Disgusting," Gulliver said. "To think that, if I'd
been born an Italian, I might be living in the Vatican,
looking after a few old walls and ceilings and things
for the Pope."

Appleby shook his head.

"My dear Gulliver," he replied, "you might have
the Brera, and be compelled to exist in Milan. Or be
living out your life in Urbino. They've a nice little
gallery, but I don't think you'd care for their winters."

"No, no—it would have to be Rome. Have you ever
wintered in Rome?" Gulliver was leading the way over
stretches of obscure mosaic in the direction of the
smoking room. "I never have. And that's positively
absurd. I might be a damned civil servant."

"But haven't you spent years in Italy?"

"Of course I have." Gulliver was whimsically impatient. "How do you think I learned my job? But
I tell you I've never spent a winter in Rome."

"You'd find it overrated, I don't doubt. Better just
to read about it in a nostalgic way in Edwardian
novels. The reality would be disenchanting. I understand there's a great deal of snow, and that the natives
have never studied to accommodate their lives to it.
Moreover in winter Rome is full of Romans, just as in
spring London is full of Londoners. And you know how
tiresome that is. No capital city is tolerable except
when voided of its inhabitants."

Sir Gabriel Gulliver received this with appropriate
amusement. Entering the smoking-room, he dived into

a corner to ring a bell, and then returned to Appleby, still mildly laughing.

"Nice of you," he said, "to talk to an old buffer in what you conceive of as his own antique conversational mode. A good many of you youngsters, you know, have no conversation at all. . . . Turned fifty yet?"

"I'm fifty-three."

"Precisely. A youngster in my regard, you may well believe."

The arrival of a servant relieved Appleby for a moment from the necessity of keeping up this badinage. Gulliver was making some rather particular enquiries about Madeira. It was possible that the great gallery over which he presided had no retiring age for its Director, and he might well be on the farther side of sixty-five. His pose as an old dodderer, however, was merely an amiable affectation. He was in the prime at least of his intellectual powers, and there were wide stretches of art history in which he was still far ahead of any up-and-coming younger men. Appleby didn't know him very well, despite Judith's obscure cousinship with him. But he had always found him entertaining. Perhaps it was only to entertain him that Gulliver had yanked him out of the reading-room now.

"And you?" Gulliver demanded, when the man had gone away. "Wouldn't *you* have been born an Italian?"

"To be Chief of Police in your blessed Rome, and spend my days investigating—or being told I was failing to investigate—monstrous orgies in high life? No, no, Gulliver. Give me London—with all its traffic problems, and with every acre of its stupid crime and squalid vice."

For a moment Gulliver was silent. He was quick to catch a tone. And when the Madeira arrived, he made an easy change of subject.

"I hope Judith is well? She hasn't been in the Gallery lately. Or she hasn't, at least, looked in on me. When she does, it's a habit I take kindly in her. I like reminiscing about dear old Luke and Everard."

"She's very well, thank you." It was a point in Gulliver's favour with Appleby that he had been on terms of some intimacy with Judith's variously gifted if crazy family. "Only she's modelling something rather intricate. Spends her days knocking up maquettes and shoving them about like a kid with toy soldiers."

"Ah, you always take that philistine tone about the poor girl's stuff. Actually, it disguises your vast admiration."

Appleby was amused.

"Well, yes," he said. "It does."

"And quite right, too. She's getting better and better. We must have a dinner, or something, and launch a move to have the Arts Council make a pet of her. Don't you think?"

"No, I don't." Appleby didn't resent this airy nonsense. "But you'd better make your kind suggestion to her."

"Of course, Judith is a shade on the traditional side. All those stones with holes through. Erosion, I'm told, has definitely gone out. *Fuori*, as our Italian friends express it. And corrosion is correspondingly in. *Dentro*. Do you know, there's a Lapp who's discovered a rapid process for corroding and encrusting barbed wire? He's done a perfectly superb Madonna in it. You can see it somewhere off Bond Street, any day, by paying no more than a mere half-crown."

"I saw it last week. And we had the Lapp to dinner. Judith made me read an article on something called Anti-Art, in order that we might have a topic for rational conversation. But the Lapp, for all his rebarbative barbed wire, hadn't heard of Anti-Art. In fact he confessed an interest in the Pre-Raphaelites. Not what you might call an informed interest. But still —there it was. I don't find artists less perplexing as I grow old."

"Nor should I—doubtless—if I ever met any. But, of course, since I got away from that damned hole on the river, I converse only with the dead. Do you know, my dear Appleby, I believe I shall end up with the same creed as Bernard Shaw's preposterous painter, in that play about doctors? I forget his name. Something like Tit for Tat."

"Dubedat."

"Precisely. And he dies on the stage, you remember, after announcing that he believes in Michael Angelo, Velasquez and Rembrandt. And I'm blessed if I don't agree with him."

Sir Gabriel Gulliver paused, and took a considering sip of his Madeira.

"As a matter of fact," he said, "it's about Rembrandt that I want to talk to you."

Appleby felt familiar with this kind of approach. Almost, he'd thought he was being subjected to it only that afternoon by Charles Gribble. There are levels of

English society in which nearly all professional advice is picked up free. Cabinet ministers murmur their symptoms negligently into the ear of distinguished consultant physicians when the ladies have withdrawn from the dinner-table. Leading Queen's Counsel know precisely what lies ahead of them when they find themselves on the right hand of brilliant and frequently dis-married hostesses. Top-ranking architects, summoned to indigestible feasts in ancient colleges, commonly take the precaution of bringing a junior staff with them and lodging them in an adjacent hotel.

But for all this sort of seeking after knowledge there is at least a substantial pool of authorities to draw on. Only one man runs London's police. He has, it is true, a large number of competent assistants. But these are not, somehow, persons largely current in society. The Archbishop of Canterbury—Appleby sometimes felt—had distinctly the advantage of him. He had all those bishops—to say nothing of his brother of York.

"Rembrandt?" It was with well-practised civil interest that Appleby repeated the name. And he picked up his glass of Madeira, wondering just what it was going to work out at in terms of expenditure of time.

"Well, yes—Rembrandt, more or less. It's a rather delicate position, as a matter of fact. Not an affair which, at the moment, I'd like to have bruited abroad."

Silence is observed.

"Do tell me," Appleby said. It couldn't be maintained that this little talk wasn't running true to form.

"People keep on bringing pictures," Sir Gabriel Gulliver pursued. "One can't very well have them simply turned away. So we run what is in fact a free-advice bureau. You read about it in the papers at times. And I've got it pretty well taped nowadays. One or another of my young men is available right through working hours. It doesn't teach them all that much about painting, but it does help them to a little knowledge about human nature. And my sort of young man needs anything of that kind that he can pick up, the Lord knows."

"Remote aesthetes, are they?" Appleby asked. "What Kipling calls long-haired things with velvet collar-rolls?"

"There you go on your philistine note again. But it's true that some of them could do with a little common humanity. Well, old ladies come in with Arundel prints, or with shiny oleographic reproductions of the Laughing Cavalier or the Night Watch, manufactured in Leipzig in the eighteen-eighties. And my lads have to explain that the blessed thing is delightful to possess, but that the market isn't precisely buoyant just at the moment. It's a point of honour that the old ladies should go away feeling rather pleased, despite their dreams of sudden wealth being unrealized."

Appleby nodded.

"Rather," he said, "like being in Complaints in a big store. The customer takes the article away again, feeling he's had a thoroughly square deal after all."

"Just so. The analogy's rather a commercial one, but fair enough. Except that we do always have the chance of a real find. All the young men believe that one day Great-grandfather's Dobbin will actually prove to be by Stubbs."

"Or Great-grandfather himself be by Lawrence or Hoppner."

"Well, even Hoppner would be something. Only it doesn't happen. It just doesn't happen at all."

"Never?" Appleby was mildly surprised.

"Next to never, anyway. It's an odd thing, but there it is. Of course finds are made, even in England, from time to time. But not from among the treasuries of the simpler classes—who are naturally the people who do most of the walking up our steps. When your impoverished country gentleman starts hopefully turning out his attics, he usually begins by sending photographs of anything likely looking to the big sale-room chaps. And if he elicits a cautious expression of interest from them, he forks out for a regular expertise. So our little public service, as I've said, isn't precisely a prolific field of art-world drama. In fact, we've never made the headlines yet. But are we going to, tomorrow or the next day? That's my headache at the moment. As you can see, I'm a worried man."

Appleby found that he wasn't disposed to question this. Gulliver, although talking with a great air of urbanity and leisure, did somehow suggest an underlying uneasiness of mind.

"You can't be worried, surely, simply because a real find has turned up at last?"

Gulliver shook his head.

"Not because it has turned up. Because it has disappeared again."

"A Rembrandt?"

"Yes. It sounds incredible. But there it is. A girl walked in with the thing last Friday."

"An unknown Rembrandt?"

"An unknown Rembrandt. And an unknown girl."

"Well, I can see that it could have been pretty startling. But there must be a great many Rembrandts in the world. Didn't he live to a respectable old age, and go on painting like mad?" Appleby paused, and received an abstracted nod from Gulliver. "This was a *good* Rembrandt?"

"Most Rembrandts aren't at all bad." Gulliver was momentarily acrid. "And of course I'm not a critic. Nor is my young man, Jimmy Heffer. We're just humble art historians. But we knew we were looking at an important Rembrandt, if that's any use to you. Perhaps you know the Old Man in the Pitti? 1658, I seem to remember. Well, this was another Old Man, and very close to that one. Not such a large canvas, mind you, but almost the same amount of paint got on to it."

Appleby smiled.

"That's a virtue?"

"It's one of the old boy's very great virtues. Painters adore him for it. And this girl walked in with a transcendent instance of it tucked under her arm."

"I see. But just what girl?"

"We don't know. We don't know at all. By the way, I think I'll change my mind. I think I'll commit myself to the statement that this was *quite* a good Rembrandt —as good as you'll find in London, Edinburgh or

Glasgow. Yes, I'd go as far as that. And this unknown girl walked in and out with it. But perhaps I'm boring you, my dear chap?"

Appleby shook his head. He wasn't exactly breathless. But he had been stirred to mild curiosity.

"Tell me the whole thing," he said.

CHAPTER THREE

"THE TROUBLE PRECISELY is that there's uncommonly little to tell."

Sir Gabriel Gulliver glanced into his empty glass as if considering its replenishment. Then he appeared to think better of this, and went on talking.

"But I can begin by explaining the drill. When a person turns up with a picture in this way, the first thing they have to do is to write their name and address in a book. Then they're asked to hand over the picture, and told that the expert will see them and give an opinion as soon as he's completed his examination. Sometimes they're unwilling to let their treasure out of their hands. But the word 'expert' usually fixes that. Have you noticed how the newspapers have made it a term of awe? There's an expert in every damned thing nowadays, and it's our duty to take what he tells us as gospel."

Appleby nodded.

"Very true. But why this business of handing over the picture or whatever?"

"Largely because people are so talkative, my dear fellow. They want to tell you that Grannie remembered the picture as a girl, so that it must be very old and therefore very valuable. That sort of thing. And we naturally don't want all that. What we want is two or three minutes with the canvas undisturbed. After that, we know just what to say when the owner is shown in on us. If the time of my young men—and my own time occasionally—is not to be consumed by this rather futile activity, the technique has to be streamlined in that way. And that was how it happened last Friday."

"First the Rembrandt and then the girl?"

"Just that. Or, more precisely, first Jimmy Heffer, then the Rembrandt, then myself, and then the girl. I don't suppose you've met Heffer?"

Appleby reflected.

"His name seems familiar."

"That's because he's an athlete. Some sort of champion at running the four hundred metres. Or is it the four thousand? Anyway, it's something out of the ordinary in my sort of young man. Not a long-haired thing." Gulliver paused, as if something had suddenly struck him. "Do you know, I believe the girl felt that about Jimmy? Not what she'd expected."

"Fell for him, you mean?"

"I'm not sure that she didn't. I had a kind of feeling they were surprising each other."

"Is this Jimmy Heffer sound at his job? Will he make a good curator of pictures and so forth?"

"Dear me, yes. Jimmy has taste, which is quite useful, and a first-class visual memory, which is the really vital thing. He'll do very well."

"Private means, I suppose?" Involuntarily, Appleby found himself asking the routine questions. "Picture galleries and museums, I imagine, scarcely offer royal roads to fortune."

"Indeed they don't. And Jimmy has something. Not much—but enough to get him about the world, and let him buy his own books and photographs. Commercial background. Family in tea, I seem to remember. No learned or academic tradition. No artistic one either. But young Jimmy is quite reasonably presentable. Winchester and New College. Or was it Eton and King's? I forget. But that sort of thing."

"I see. And was this girl with the Rembrandt Winchester and New College too?"

"Well, yes—if you want to put it that way. Perfect young gentlewoman, and all that. But let me get back to telling you the story in an orderly fashion. On Friday morning this picture was brought in to Heffer. Wrapped in brown paper, and on its stretcher, although without its frame. Jimmy took one look at it—or it may have been two—and tumbled across the corridor into my room. Didn't so much as knock at the door."

"Natural, even for a Wykehamist. In the exciting circumstances, that's to say."

"Quite so. Well, I went back to his room with him. And there was this thing. This utterly monumental thing."

"A *good* Rembrandt."

"Just that. Jimmy had propped it up on his table, opposite the window. For a moment I thought it was the St. Paul from the Widener Collection in Philadelphia. I believe I turned on Jimmy almost indignantly, and demanded how the devil he'd got hold of *that*. Then I realized it was a portrait I'd never seen —nor ever seen reproduced. But still, of course, it never occurred to me that it could simply have been trundled in on us in the way it was—straight off the street, as you might say."

"But you were instantly certain"—Appleby glanced curiously at his companion—"that it was an authentic portrait by Rembrandt?"

"Lord, yes. Not a doubt of it."

"I ask because there's a devilish lot of high-class forgery and faking about. I ran into something of the kind in this very club only a few hours ago."

"Is that so?" Gulliver didn't seem interested. "Well, there was no doubt about this. A layman might suppose we'd have to make refined scientific tests before we could exclude the possibility of forgery. But that's all my eye. Or *sometimes* it's all my eye. And this was one of the times. All the photographic and chemical jiggery-pokery was ready to lay on next door, of course. And Jimmy Heffer himself was competent to do some of the latest things. But there was just no need for them. We *knew*."

"Most impressive," Appleby said. "But I wonder why? Might it conceivably be because this good Rembrandt was a *very* good Rembrandt?"

Gulliver laughed rather shortly. It was as if he was suddenly impatient with the whimsical tone he had imported into his own narrative.

"Yes, yes. And there we were, the two of us, staring at the thing. And Jimmy telling me that he understood it had been brought in by a woman, and asking me if I would please take charge. Do you know, I had positively to wrench my attention back to the youth? The junk I live among is pretty comprehensively of the highest class, I think you'll agree. I oughtn't to have been all that staggered by the appearance of just one more pebble on the vast shore of the world's art. And yet I was goggling at the fatness of that impasto as if it were an absolutely new revelation to me. It was the unexpectedness of the incident, no doubt, that made the experience so vivid. Would you care for another glass of that Madeira? I don't consider it positively bad."

Appleby pushed away his glass.

"I think not, thank you. And then you had in the young gentlewoman?"

"We had her in—as soon as I'd taken breath and given the situation a little thought. You see, it didn't lack its tricky side."

"Connected with the fact that the picture was worth a lot of money?"

"Certainly. The picture-market is a crackpot affair, as you know. And never more so than of late, with ignoramuses pouring out meaningless money for Impressionists and Post-Impressionists and what-have-you. But even poor old Rembrandt hasn't quite had his day. This thing—propped up before us by Jimmy Heffer's bowler hat—would fetch almost as much under the hammer as anything that hung on the walls of the building we were gorping and gaping in."

"I can't imagine you doing anything so inelegant," Appleby said.

"I assure you I was doing exactly that. And it's all very well, you know, telling any casual caller that their picture's really very pretty, and undoubtedly painted by hand. You can even be quite light-hearted about saying it looks as if they've got hold of an Etty or a Maclise. But when it comes to a woman strolling in with a shattering Old Master, a little circumspection is probably wise. Before I gave a formal opinion, for example, the routine sort of tests ought to be made, even although I knew they were superfluous. And I ought to know something about the thing's provenance."

"That would be wise, even in quite minor affairs." Appleby was thinking of poor Charles Gribble's discomfiture over Manallace.

"Exactly. And I ought to satisfy myself that this enquiry about the Rembrandt was being made by, or with the sanction of, the legal owner. All this was fairly elementary, but it took me a moment or two to get it clear in my head before I told Jimmy to ring his bell and have the lady in."

Gulliver paused, and Appleby glanced round the smoking room. His friend's voice was silvery and resonant, so that anybody might be having the benefit of this odd story. But in fact they were quite alone.

"It must have been an interesting moment," Appleby said. "The entrance of the proprietor of this rather tremendous object."

"Well, yes. But—do you know?—I was still so absorbed in the tremendous object itself that it was seconds before I looked round when the door opened. And, even then, it wasn't the woman I found myself looking at. It was Jimmy. And the way *he* was looking made the moment not so much interesting as laughable. He had gorped and gaped, as I said, at the Old Man, just as I had. But he was in a very ecstasy of gorping and gaping now. I remarked—didn't I?—that the lad had taste. Well, it was getting at him. Rembrandt had been knocked clean out of his head. And you might say that Botticelli had taken his place."

"Botticelli?"

"Yes, indeed. The girl, you see, was quite astounding. One looked at once for dancing waves and a great scallop shell under her feet. One found something positively improbable in the fact that she had clothes on."

"Dear me!"

"But you mustn't suppose me to mean that there was anything lascivious about her. It was just that she had that sort of beauty. *Precisely* that sort of beauty. She had stepped from the walls of the Ufizzi, you might say, and slipped into a well-made coat and skirt."

Appleby vindicated the philistinism which Gulliver had earlier attributed to him by finding this funny. In fact he threw back his head and laughed.

"Quite so, quite so." Gulliver laughed too. "But there it was. The birth of Venus."

Appleby shook his head more soberly.

"I don't believe it," he said. "Botticelli's lady is undoubtedly pleasing as a bit of paint. But she's not remotely human. She's as weightless as a space traveller. And, if there's ballet on Mount Olympus, hers is a ballerina mask."

"No doubt. I'm talking at random, I don't deny. An old fellow, you know, rather whips up feelings about those things—a girl's face, and so on—when he knows he's a bit beyond them."

Appleby said nothing to this, and the consequence was a moment's pause. There was something frustrated or baffled, he was thinking, beneath Gulliver's urbanity. He was a man not reconciled to the direction in which life had taken him. And perhaps a woman had started the trouble long ago.

"And indeed," Gulliver went on, "I'm testifying to something against my own convictions. I don't believe that there is anything that can be called feminine beauty in an absolute sense. It's only some informing —and perhaps evanescent—sensibility which makes any lass worth looking at twice. So let us pass on. Here was a really striking girl, we'll say. And here was my young athlete struck all of a heap by her. Naturally it fell to me to do the talking. And that was just as well. Jimmy Heffer, I'm convinced, couldn't have uttered a word."

"This didn't work the other way round as well? The young person wasn't struck all of a heap by the athlete?"

"Well, as I think I said, I had a feeling that they were surprising each other. I'd say she found Jimmy more unexpected than she found me. Her notion of the sort of person who looks after pictures would be quite conventional. But remember that I wasn't in on their first glance at each other. I was still looking at the picture."

"Yes, I see." Appleby thought for a moment. "What sort of girl was she—apart from this Aphrodite aspect?"

"A well-bred girl, but far from sophisticated. Indeed she was shy and rather awkward."

"An awkward Aphrodite? That's rather disappointing, I'm bound to say."

"She was in a novel situation. And, when she spoke, she was composed enough. She apologized for bothering us, and hoped it wasn't entirely out of order. That sort of thing. I asked her to sit down, and thanked her for bringing the picture along. I said it interested me very much, and I asked her whether she herself had any idea of who might have painted it. She seemed to hesitate. And then she said no, but it did seem to her that it might be very old. At that young Heffer chipped in—rather abruptly and dogmatically for him. He said the picture was very probably within a month or two of its three hundredth birthday."

"And how did the young lady take that?"

"She looked at Jimmy almost as if she were scared of him. I suppose she regarded such precision as a sort of black magic. Then I asked her a question which seemed perfectly legitimate in itself, but which certainly scared her a good deal more."

"Whether she owned the thing?"

"I didn't put it exactly that way. I asked her whether it had been in her family a long time. She looked at me with all the grave candour of that Botticelli face—but I had a strong impression that she didn't, for a moment, know what to reply. Then she said: 'Oh, yes—we haven't just bought it, or anything like that.'"

Sir Gabriel Gulliver had paused in his narrative, and Appleby took a moment before asking a question.

"There was a point, it seems, at which you became uneasy about the whole business. Was this it?"

"I think it was. And I think that Jimmy Heffer was uneasy too. He was refraining from looking at the girl, as if he didn't want to give the appearance of challenging her. For my own part, and in spite of her charms, I felt we'd better get rid of her, and think a little. So I said the picture might well be by Rembrandt——"

"Did that register? She'd heard of him?"

"Oh, yes. She was a simple girl, no doubt, but not to the extent of being utterly without ordinary information. I said that we didn't, however, care to make a positive statement at once, and that she had better leave the canvas for thorough examination. Then I explained our procedure in such cases. We take a photograph straight away, and have a print within ten minutes. On the back of the print there's a form of receipt, with the conditions upon which we accept works of art for preliminary gratuitous expertise. Our trustees' legal advisers insist on that."

Appleby nodded approvingly.

"Businesslike," he said. "You certainly have it streamlined, as you said."

"It was too businesslike, it seems, for our young person. Aphrodite looked thoroughly alarmed. But that was only for a moment. Then she recovered her self-possession—something which, in fact, she abundantly rejoiced in. She thanked us, said that she required no more formal opinion, walked over to the Old Man, and quite coolly wrapped him up again in his brown paper. Then she simply gave us her grave smile—with an extra tilt of the chin, I felt, for Jimmy—and walked out, picture and all. Of course, I hadn't the slightest title to prevent her."

There was another pause. Gulliver had sat back with elegantly folded hands. It appeared that the main part of his narrative was over, and that Appleby was now expected to offer appropriate comment.

"Interesting," Appleby said. "And tantalizing, no doubt. How old was this girl?"

"A mere child. Twenty-one or twenty-two."

"Town or country?"

"A rural Venus, I was inclined to suppose. Schooling which was mostly ponies and a home which was mostly spaniels. Parents who had returned from some modest imperial station to some equally modest hereditary plot. Some small upper-middle class ambience of that sort, with nothing remarkable to it except those almost preternaturally good looks of the girl herself. That was my guess—and I remember offering it to Heffer there and then. He said that I was very probably right, but that we could at least begin from a basis of established fact. And he rang his bell and had in the visitors' book. I'd clean forgotten it. But of course the girl had written her name in it. Astarte Oakes."

Appleby raised his eyebrows.

"Do people of the pony and spaniel order go in for that sort of fancy christian name?"

Gulliver nodded confidently.

"Dear me, yes. All sorts of mad names. I've often remarked it."

"Even if their surname is Oakes?"

"Certainly. Oakes or Nokes or Stokes—it makes no matter."

"And there was an address?"

"Yes—and, although it wasn't very informative, it seemed to support the rural Venus theory. It was a hotel in Bloomsbury. One of those largish unassuming places one's never been in. Full, I imagine, of bed-and breakfasting families from Wigan and Glasgow."

"That doesn't seem quite to fit, after all."

"No more it *did* fit, as you'll presently hear. I said I was worried, didn't I? Well, the worrying began almost straight away. There was surely something odd about a girl drifting round with hundreds of thousands of pounds worth of art under her arm—to say nothing of its being an infernally good picture. I tried to think what such a state of affairs could all be about. I imagined some condition of pretty severe poverty."

"Did the girl's clothes suggest that?"

"Well, no—I can't say they did. But these things are relative, after all. I imagined the father—a retired colonial governor, you know—dead, and mummy and the girl living with some terribly gaga and unreasonable old grandfather. And the ponies having to be sold and the spaniels going mangy and the drawing-room chintzes in tatters and the gardener crippled with rheumatism and the garden-boy demanding a man's wage and——"

Appleby mildly interrupted.

"I think I have the idea, my dear fellow."

"And mother and daughter putting their heads together and remembering this old picture—and perhaps remembering, too, something some knowledgeable guest may have said about it—and then the girl's saying that she'll jolly well find out. Something of that sort, eh? Her expedition not really an authorized one, but at the same time entirely innocent. The conjecture I built up was roughly like that."

"It's most convincing. You know, Gulliver, it occurs to me that you ought to have been a novelist."

"Do you really think so?" Gulliver seemed pleased.

"As a matter of fact, I have sometimes thought that, at a pinch, my imagination could contrive pretty well."

"Or a detective." Appleby glanced curiously at his eminent friend. "You would make a detective, without a doubt."

"Wait, my boy, wait! There's real sleuthing to come. I visited that hotel."

Appleby stared.

"Now you do surprise me. Very much."

"I surprised myself. But the incident had gone on bothering me, and I felt I ought not simply to let it drop. Of course it was, in a sense, no longer any business of mine. We'd done what we hold ourselves out as offering to do, and if I chased up that Rembrandt I might fairly be called a busybody. But it was undoubtedly an important picture."

"And worth all that money. For my own part"— and Appleby glanced at Gulliver in what might have been whimsical apology—"I think I'd have felt the simple vulgar fascination of that."

"Quite so, quite so. It was very much in my mind that the girl mightn't have formed an accurate notion of that. I decided I'd feel easier if she—or whoever she was in one way or another acting for—had a written communication from us. Or perhaps I was just curious. Anyway, I went to that hotel yesterday morning. Perhaps it wasn't exactly dignified. But who cares about that?"

"Who, indeed? And I'm sure you could carry off any mild awkwardness there might be."

"Very handsome of you to say so, Appleby. Well, I decided I'd ask for the girl, although she would almost certainly be gone. They'd be bound to have her home address. If it turned out that I couldn't simply ask for it with an adequate appearance of propriety, I could at least get them to forward a letter. But all this was a miscalculation. The hotel had never heard of Astarte Oakes. They looked back through their register for a full fortnight. There was no trace of her."

Appleby made no attempt to receive this denouement with astonishment.

"And that's where the matter now stands?" he asked.

"More or less. But I've discovered one other thing. If it *is* a discovery. I have a colleague called Mountford, who has made something of a hobby of graphology. Would you ever have heard of him?"

"Lord, yes! It's a good deal more than a hobby. He's a recognized authority on handwriting. I've heard him give expert evidence in court."

"Well, this morning it occurred to me to show Mountford our visitors' book. He took one look at 'Astarte Oakes' and declared it wasn't the writer's real name. He was quite persuasive about it. He said it had been written by somebody who had suddenly been required to do something unexpected, and that the writing betrayed the writer as making up the name as she wrote. What do you think of that?"

"I've very little doubt that Mountford's right. To his sort of eye, any true signature has a character that will be missing from any other written name. Your Astarte Oakes made up Astarte Oakes on the spot. By the way, wasn't it the opinion of some that Astarte and Aphrodite were the same divinity? I think your lass has a very good notion of the impression she makes." Appleby paused. "And—again by the way—doesn't your young Jimmy Heffer rather fade out of the story? I'd have expected you to make him do the chasing round."

"Jimmy? He went on holiday the day after the girl called on us. He had about ten days saved up."

"I see. And he'd given you whatever sort of notice you expect about holidays?"

"Well, no. There was just a scribble from him in the morning. I keep everything of that sort very casual, you know. We're a small group of intimate colleagues, and even with the quite junior people it seems the right note to maintain. So it wasn't entirely out of the way. Still, I confess that I was just a little surprised. Particularly as Jimmy said nothing about where he was going off to. He's usually a very friendly, as well as an impeccably civil, lad."

"Well, well." Again Appleby paused. "Isn't what you're really confessing something rather different? To be quite honest, Gulliver, haven't you got it in your head that your young man has gone off after the false Astarte—and may in consequence be getting himself into mischief?"

"It seems very absurd, I know." Sir Gabriel Gulliver seemed almost embarrassed at owning to the trend of his thoughts. "But there it is. You've hit the nail on the head. And I can't even decide whether I suppose Jimmy to be after the girl or after the picture."

"Might it be both? Heffer seems to be a connoisseur. And here are two articles which, if you're to be believed, are both quite first-class in their line."

"It might be both, no doubt. Jimmy might feel that the girl and her picture go together. But, whether that's the way of it or not, I do feel that the whole matter ought to be—well, investigated."

Appleby looked rather grimly at his companion.

"I'm surprised," he said drily, "that you don't appeal to the police."

"I don't know that I could do that. Not, that is to say, officially, my dear chap. After all, one hasn't any suspicion of a crime. Or has one?"

Appleby shook his head. He had quite ceased to respond to Gulliver with any appearance of pleasantry. Moreover he now took out his watch and glanced at it.

"It's my unfortunate business," he said, "always to be suspecting crimes. Or it was until I became rather a busy administrator. You're not seriously proposing, are you, that I should myself go chasing after these people, or that picture?"

Gulliver rose to his feet.

"No, no," he said urbanely. "I know you have your hands full of weightier matters. But I have an obscure feeling, as I've tried to hint, that this matter is *delicate*. And *interesting*. Even, conceivably, *odd*. In short, my dear Appleby, very much what used to be your sort of thing. A long time ago, of course."

"Quite so," Appleby said drily. "When I was at the height, you might have added, of such modest but useful powers as I possessed."

Gulliver laughed easily.

"Come, come," he said. "I don't think I'd care to cross swords with you, my dear man, even in your present self-declared decrepitude. As for my Rembrandt and so on—just give it a thought or two. No more than that." Gulliver moved to the door. "Dining?"

Appleby shook his head.

"I'm going home. We've guests, I think."

"Then, good evening to you." Gulliver paused at the door. "By the way, you'd *like* it—that Rembrandt, I mean—if you ever—um—ran it to earth. It's terrific. My love to Judith, please."

CHAPTER FOUR

It was an axiom of Appleby's that nobody can possibly live through a London day without being badly in need of a bath before dinner, and he remained unimpressed before his wife's contention that this was merely a genteel superstition, to which 98 per cent. of the metropolitan population rose superior every evening. It wasn't, Appleby would explain, just a matter of the physical dirt with which the place systematically encrusted one. Such intellectual pores as an ageing drudge still possessed had to be unclogged too. He got into his bath with a dozen of the day's issues continuing to scurry round in his head. When he got out of it they had either all departed for ever, or they had all so departed except one, which thus stood revealed as really meriting a little further thinking about. Not that it continued to make that claim there and then, for as the bath-water drained away it regularly vanished too. But it had, somehow, made its mark, and occasionally it consented to painless elucidation during the slumbers of the succeeding night.

And there was no guessing beforehand which of many matters might thus survive ablution. In the course of this very day, for instance, he had read several reports on issues of serious moment. It was hard not to feel at the end of them that London, as a civilized city, pretty well had its back to the wall. In face of them, certainly, Sir Gabriel Gulliver's yarn ought to have faded at a first grab at the soap. Yet here it was, spot-lit in Appleby's mind, and the whole of the rest of a busy day blotted out.

"Judith," Appleby called, "I've got a message for you."

Lady Appleby appeared at the bathroom door. She had the abstracted and slightly forbidding air natural in a much-occupied professional woman and housewife who must, within the next fifteen minutes, transform herself into a leisured hostess in the Edwardian mode.

"A message, John? Is it something you ought to have remembered as soon as you got in?"

"Oh, no—nothing like that. Just that old Gulliver sends you his love."

Judith, who had been distracted from a crucial operation before a looking-glass, made a resigned noise and turned back into her bedroom.

"Nice of him," she called back. "Old habit, of course. Gabriel Gulliver has been sending his love to women for half a century—and drawing lucky from time to time."

Appleby lay back in water that was agonizingly hot. In the early hours of that morning an eighteen-year-old Stepney lad, having unfortunately been rather heavily shod when feeling entitled to the contents of an elderly shopkeeper's till, had taken a first and certain step in the direction of the gallows. Appleby always made the water hotter, somehow, when anything of that kind had occurred.

"Dear me!" he said. "I think of Gulliver as a respectable old connection and family friend. Your uncles were devoted to him. Are you suggesting he has been a person of irregular life?"

Judith gave a shout of laughter. It was delighted laughter, because in the looking-glass things were coming right.

"John, dear, your way of expressing yourself is getting nearer and nearer to that of a High Court judge. Gabriel Gulliver has been a restless and unsatisfied person all his days. And he was tiresome with women."

"Well, well. Perhaps he's being tiresome about you. He says you don't call in on him in his blessed gallery. You don't mean to say he's been making improper advances to you?"

"It would be inconceivable, wouldn't it?" Judith appeared in the bathroom door again, carrying a necklace. "Fasten this, will you? I must go down and see that everything isn't chaos. Was old Gabriel entertaining?"

"He had an extraordinary yarn about an unknown Rembrandt which is being carried around by a girl calling herself Astarte Oakes."

"Good. You can tell it at dinner. It sounds just right for the Bendixsons."

"It's more or less confidential, I'm afraid. I'll tell you about it afterwards. Who else is coming, besides the Bendixsons?"

But Judith, having got her necklace to rights, had vanished. Appleby went into his dressing-room. He was rummaging for a shirt when the telephone rang. It was the routine report he always received at this hour. For two or three minutes he listened to the precise voice from the other end, only now and then interrupting with a brief direction. Finally he asked a question.

"And that Stepney affair? There's no doubt that the lad took the money?"

"None at all, sir, I'm afraid." The voice would have been slightly impatient if it hadn't been perfectly correct.

"I had my mind on the lodger upstairs—the old man with the petty criminal record. It seemed to me just possible that, immediately after the killing, he might have taken advantage of the confusion to help himself from the till."

"Yes, sir. The possibility has been very fully investigated."

"If that were the way of it, then the lad's motive might not have been robbery at all. The old woman might have refused him credit."

"It would remain a poor reason for kicking someone to death, sir."

"I don't need to be told that, Parsons." Appleby snapped this out in a tone he didn't often use. "We have to consider the interest of the accused man, you know, in the existing state of the law."

"Yes, sir. But we found nearly six pounds on him. And, only a couple of hours before, he'd struck his mother because she wouldn't let him have half-a-crown. He's a very violent lad—and perhaps a bit crazy. The defence will be more interested in diminished responsibility than in that old man upstairs."

"Very well, Parsons." Appleby's voice was briskly approving again. "Anything else?"

"I don't think so, sir. Another probable homicide—in Bloomsbury this time. Fellow calling himself an antiquarian bookseller. Would you like particulars now?"

Appleby glanced at his watch.

"No. But send me up a note about it tomorrow. And thank you, Parsons. Good-night."

Appleby put down the receiver and reached for a black tie. People who got themselves murdered, whether in Stepney or Bloomsbury, were no longer any very direct concern of his. If a corpse ever came his way now, it was only after having passed, so to speak, through a beautiful electric type-writer and then having been analysed under half a dozen intelligently chosen headings. It had been better fun when he had dealt with them in the raw. And sometimes they had been very much that.

When Appleby opened the drawing-room door he saw that someone had already arrived. So he entered with an air of cheerful apology which he maintained while Judith introduced him to Mary Wildsmith. He was sure he had never seen her before, and almost sure he had never heard of her. She was old rather than young, and small rather than large—and at a first glance one would probably have ventured that there was nothing more to be said about her. For her face couldn't be held to possess features, nor her voice character—so that all in all she seemed to Appleby, as he poured her sherry, to be pretty well the essence of the unmemorable. This made it the more annoying that Judith had presented him to this stranger with a total lack of explanations coupled with the largest suggestion that it was a moment in which one of her husband's longest cherished ambitions was being realized.

"It's frightfully good of you," Appleby said, "to find time to come to dinner with us. You must be tremendously busy and tremendously in demand."

Miss Wildsmith—for she seemed to be that—was amused. And it was in a fashion, somehow, that told Appleby at once that she was a clever woman. Moreover as her amusement took the form of a momentary and entirely deliberate transformation of her neutral expression into one of extraordinary mobility and charm, he realised that at least he had got hold of her profession. And at once Judith, who had tumbled to his blankness before Miss Wildsmith's name, confirmed this.

"Mary's last enchanting part," she said, "was as the Hungarian refugee in *Thunder Without Rain*."

Appleby registered appropriate enlightenment.

"Yes, indeed," he said. "Everybody talked of it. I was extremely sorry not to see it."

"But your wife says you *did* see it." Mary Wildsmith again looked amused. But this time she looked, so to speak, like a different person being amused. She was a character actress, one must suppose, who enjoyed moving freely around.

Appleby nodded easily. If Judith said he had seen *Thunder Without Rain* then, no doubt, he *had* seen it. But it appeared to him absurd to expect any rational being to remember one West End play from another.

"Only the first act," he said firmly. "Most unfortunately, I was called out of the theatre. So the last

time I really had the pleasure of seeing you"—a
genuine flash of memory about Mary Wildsmith had
seemed to come to him amid all this nonsense—"was
as the Countess of Rousillon in *All's Well*. It must have
been at the Old Vic."

"We're a theatrical family," Miss Wildsmith said.
"And that was my aunt." She held out her empty
glass. "But your sherry, Sir John, makes up for a
great deal."

It was at this moment—and rather to Appleby's
relief—that the Bendixsons arrived. He did at least
know Carl Bendixson and his wife Gretta, and they
were entirely estimable people. Bendixson was an
auctioneer—but an auctioneer of the exalted sort who
banged his hammer over the heads of Maillol bronzes
and Renoir nudes. His wife was a painter of dazzling
technique and—as far as Appleby knew—very little
else. The Bendixsons lived in a much grander way than
the Applebys did. Hammer-banging, after all, had been
booming for years. But Judith was ahead of Gretta
Bendixson as an artist favoured by the well-informed.
And that no doubt evened things up. As Appleby
handed the Bendixsons the sherry of which Mary
Wildsmith approved, he was quite clear in his mind
that *they* wouldn't approve of it. Or not, that was to
say, as an offering that could appropriately be com-
mented on. But they were a reasonable couple, all the
same.

And, fortunately, the Bendixsons proved to be
thoroughly well clued up on this Mary Wildsmith. It
seemed that Miss Wildsmith did a good deal of resting

nowadays, but that she had quite a name for precisely what Appleby had conjectured: versatility in small character parts. At the same time, Appleby got the impression that there had been some sort of hitch in the lady's career. Perhaps, he thought, Miss Wildsmith had been a little too intelligent to fit quite comfortably into all those imbecile plays. Yes—that might very well be it.

He became aware of Judith moving a candlestick on the chimney-piece. She was doing this in order to look at the clock without appearing to do so. There could be no doubt that somebody had failed to turn up. The missing guest must be a male. And probably he was a male hitherto unknown to his host. That would be Judith's way of balancing up her party.

And the clock, it seemed, had ticked its way past some deadline. Appleby saw his wife press a bell. In fact he saw her rapidly press it twice. So at least they would now get something to eat. The Appleby domestic staff was not extensive. Apart from a person so ephemeral that it was hard not to refer to her simply as the foreign girl, it consisted of two persons almost so answeringly ephemeral that Appleby was accustomed to think of them as the decayed couple. But it was undeniable that Judith always had these impermanent appearances on their toes. Those two rings had assured that the round dinner-table would presently proclaim its expectation not of six diners but of five. The missing guest had been obliterated. No reference would be made to him. If he did now turn up, he would be received with cordiality and mild surprise. Judith's art, Appleby reflected, remained notably *avant-garde*.

But her social assumptions approximated more and more closely to those of her great-grandparents. Appleby, who didn't regard himself as possessing great-grandparents, found this very amusing. But he certainly wouldn't venture, later in this evening's proceedings, to enquire baldly as to who hadn't turned up. That would have to keep until bed-time.

"But what a heavenly thing!" Gretta Bendixson cried with amiable enthusiasm as she sat down. She was pointing at a somewhat battered object in the centre of the table. "It must be frightfully old."

"Fourteen thirty-four," Judith said briskly. "It came from a manor-house in Kent, and I traced it in *Earliest English Wills*. 'A feir salt saler of peautre with a feyre knoppe'. I don't think there's much doubt about it. Do you like the feyre knoppe?"

"Perfectly charming!" Carl Bendixson said, backing up his wife. "I really covet it. We have nothing like it ourselves. Except, perhaps, our 'sex silver spones with knopis of oure Ladie'."

"A small treasure," Gretta Bendixson said, "which we picked up in the junk shop in the tiny place, Bryne Bay, where we keep our yacht. Would anyone have believed it?"

"And oddly enough," Carl Bendixson pursued, "they're authenticated by way of the *Testamenta Eboracensia*. That seems unbelievable too. And one has to look out, where metals are concerned. The chemists and physicists can't really do much for you."

"You mean about faking?" Mary Wildsmith asked.

"Just that. Where organic substances are concerned, the fakers of really old objects have had it, you know.

There are foolproof tests which have simply given them notice to quit."

"How intensely interesting," Mary Wildsmith said.

"For instance," Bendixson went on, "it's no good happily manufacturing a *cinquecento* bridal chest out of timber that was still alive and flourishing a couple of hundred years later. It's immensely harder to get away with such things now than it was even twenty years ago. Appleby, wouldn't you agree?"

"In a general way—yes." It was with an effort that Appleby brought his mind back to this cultivated chatter. It had been drifting to a teen-age lad, nurtured and nudged by a squalid environment into mistaken notions of the function of footwear. "But ingenuity is still at work. Mummy, for instance."

"Mummy?" Mary Wildsmith repeated. She seemed momentarily at a loss—as if supposing, perhaps, that Appleby was invoking his wife in her maternal relationship.

"Human flesh, suitably embalmed and of suitable antiquity, was for long prized by painters as a source of some of the finest pigments."

"Like Sir Thomas Browne," Mary Wildsmith said. " 'To burn the bones of the Kings of Edom for lime were no irrational ferity'."

"Just that." It seemed to Appleby rather notable that a woman out of inane drawing-room comedies could produce chit-chat like this. "And the next time you look at a Titian, remember that those gorgeous expanses of flesh may have real flesh in them."

"Sir John—how utterly revolting!" Gretta Bendixson consumed a spoonful of soup with undiminished satisfaction. "And you don't mean to say that when *I* paint a nude——"

Appleby laughed.

"I imagine not—nor when Renoir did, either. But I'm sure you know far more about the chemistry of your job than I do."

"Oh, nothing at all!" Gretta Bendixson was at once airy and emphatic. "But if I were using mummy I think I'd know—just by a feeling creeping up the brush."

"People do still use it, it seems. Not long ago, I had some concern with a fellow who wanted a licence to import an Egyptian mummy. Technically, a mummy is a corpse and nothing else—which is why a licence was necessary. He said the thing was to be put in some private museum. But I have a notion that the appropriate parts of it were really going to be manufactured into pigment. Probably for one of those borderlines between restoring and faking that exist in the fine-art trade."

Bendixson nodded.

"They certainly do exist. I come across them, as you may imagine. But, in general, what I was saying a minute ago holds good. Faking or forging things supposed to have been created centuries back is for the most part now much too difficult to pay. Of course, there's a large low-class trade of the sort—larger than it ever was. There are plenty of people who want ancient-looking things, and who haven't much notion that there can be any effective check on them. They pay absurdly high prices at times, and the industry concerned is no doubt an extremely prosperous one. But it's worlds away from the territory of the real collectors."

"The people," Judith said, "you knock things down to once a week."

"Precisely. As the vulgar say, they know their onions."

"Or think they do." Appleby was remembering Charles Gribble. "But, if the successful faking of really old things has become so difficult of recent years, there is likely to be increased activity in the faking of comparatively recent ones? I've had to do with some cases of that."

"Yes, indeed."

Gretta Bendixson looked at her husband.

"Do you mean," she said, "French painters at the turn of the century, and that sort of thing?"

"Yes, darling. Just that. It's comparatively easy to bring them into being—after a fashion."

"But what fun!" Gretta Bendixson looked round the table as if to gather attention to herself. "I'd love to produce a Cézanne or two." She put down her spoon, and for a moment her right hand made comical but sensitive movements before an imaginary canvas. "And I believe I could. Oh, I believe I could!"

"I'd put nothing beyond you," her husband said humorously. "Would you, Mary?"

"I'd believe anything of Gretta. She'd even make no bones about getting going on a mummy." Mary Wildsmith spoke with cheerful conviction, and Appleby realized that these people were better known to each other than they were to their hosts. "And," Miss Wildsmith went on, "if Gretta does a Cézanne I'll make an offer for it at once. It would have what they call curious interest. It might even be valuable. Sir John, don't you agree?"

Recalling the value of Geoffrey Manallace's concoctions in the estimation of Charles Gribble and his American rivals, Appleby couldn't but agree.

"But it has always seemed to me," he said, "that parody is more interesting than forgery. It's curious that painters haven't exploited it more, if only as a critical instrument."

"Picasso has," Mary Wildsmith said. "But then Picasso has exploited everything—including Picasso."

There was appropriate laughter.

Sixty years in a little general shop, Appleby thought, and kicked to death at the end of them.

It was at the conclusion of the evening that the talk came back to forgery. And it was Mary Wildsmith who brought it up again.

"I gathered," she said, "that it's Impressionists, and people of that sort, who are counterfeited now. The reputed artist must be dead, I suppose, since otherwise he might come along and repudiate the fake. But he mustn't be too dead, because of those technical difficulties in fudging up anything that is going to claim substantial antiquity. But how does one market a bogus Cézanne? I mean, how does one account for it? One can hardly claim to have discovered it in one's grandmother's attics or cellars."

Carl Bendixson nodded.

"That's the crux of the matter," he said. "And there are some uncommonly ingenious ways of providing a fake with a respectable provenance. I've met them in the way of business, and I know."

"But how intensely interesting!" It would have been hard to tell, Appleby thought, whether Miss Wildsmith meant what she said by this formula, or was merely continuing to manufacture what might be called social noises. "*Do* tell us!" she went on.

But Bendixson shook his head. It was clear that he was going to strike his not unfamiliar humorous note.

"No, no," he said. "Tricks of the trade. It might be putting ideas in your head, Mary. And in Gretta's. Gretta as good as said she would make a marvellous forger. So I'm not going to put the ways and means in her hands. Lady Appleby, does your husband tell you tricks of the trade?"

"No. He keeps everything under his own hat. All his most exciting cases. Nobody else knows a thing until they're all over."

"How very vexing. And now Gretta's making faces at me. It must mean that we have to go home."

"A scattered sort of day," Appleby said lazily, as he came back from the front door. "A bit of this, and a bit of that, and nothing much hitching on to anything else. By the way, who was it that failed to turn up?"

"Somebody like Mary Wildsmith," Judith said. "I mean, somebody whom I think you haven't met. A

young man of Gabriel Gulliver's. His name's Jimmy
Heffer."

"How very odd!" Appleby stared at his wife. "And
he sent no word?"

"None whatever. Presumably he just forgot, and
there will be an abject letter of apology in a day or
two. The young are extremely casual nowadays."

"Yes," Appleby said. "Yes. But you see, as it
happens——"

A telephone-bell rang in a corner of the room, and
Appleby went over to the instrument and picked
it up.

"John Appleby," he said, and listened. "No, my
dear Gribble—not at all," he said. "Go ahead." There
was a pause, and Judith Appleby could hear a very
excited voice at the other end of the line. "*Murdered?*"
Appleby suddenly said. "*What* man? . . . Your little
dealer . . . the Manallace man . . . Bloomsbury? . . .
No, I've heard nothing—or rather I did hear that an
antiquarian bookseller——" He broke off, and listened
again. "Yes, of course," he said. "Good-night." And
he put down the telephone.

"What on earth was that?" Judith asked.

"Charles Gribble. It seems that some little dealer he
was telling me about this afternoon has been——"

Another bell interrupted Appleby. This time, it was
at his front door. Since the decayed couple had gone
off duty, he went to answer it himself. And, a moment
later, he was following Sir Gabriel Gulliver back into
Judith's drawing-room.

"Outrageous!" Gulliver was shouting. "Your damned
police! Some little bookseller been murdered in

Bloomsbury. And they've arrested my young man. The one I was telling you about. Jimmy Heffer."

There was a moment's silence. And then Appleby turned to his wife.

"So now we know," he said, "why we were that rather awkward number at dinner." He turned back to the telephone. "Didn't you tell me, Gulliver"—he said, as he picked it up—"that your Jimmy had taken a rather sudden holiday? We can at least find out whether he's really going to spend the tail-end of it in gaol."

Gulliver threw back his head. He was still very excited.

"Thank you," he said. "I'll be grateful for anything you can discover. But the thing astounds me. It simply doesn't make sense."

"I'll see that it soon does." Appleby had already dialled his number, and his enquiries didn't take long. He put down the receiver. "So far," he said, "your young gentleman has simply been detained. Persuaded, that is, to stay put. At least, it sounds like that."

"In this place in Bloomsbury?"

"Yes—in the dead man's shop. I'll go along and look into it now. Let Judith give you a drink, Gulliver, before you go home."

"Can't I——"

But Appleby interrupted rather brusquely.

"I don't think that my damned police, as you are pleased to call them, will want a crowd. You can trust me to see that Heffer has immediate legal advice, if it's required. And I'll let you have in the morning anything that it's proper you should know."

For a moment Sir Gabriel Gulliver looked extremely angry. Then he nodded quickly.

"I apologize," he said. "It wasn't a proper way to speak of your people. But do what you can for Jimmy."

Appleby made no reply. He had picked up the telephone again to call his car.

CHAPTER FIVE

JACOB TRECHMANN—FOR that was the dead
dealer's name—would have appeared to the casual eye
to be in a shabby as well as a small way of business.
His small shop was in a shabby street. But it was a
street opening at one end upon the majestic bulk of
the British Museum—now silhouetted against the dull
red glow of London's night sky. There was a single
small window, made yet smaller by a concave curtain
of moth-eaten grey velvet. Before this, three or four
small and ancient books were disposed, together with
a small typed card that said:

> *Incunabula from the library of
> the late Professor Ludwig von
> Zinzendorf of the University of
> Heidelberg.*

Appleby paused to peer at these treasures. The
street-lighting was indifferent, and in the little window
there was no light at all. So in fact he didn't make much
of them. But at least they had such an enormous
appearance of authenticity—of having dropped straight,
so to speak, from the press of Gutenberg or whoever—
that he was at once perversely prompted, doubtless as
a result of his massive exposure to the subject that day,
to speculate as to whether they might not in fact be
monstrous forgeries. But of course people didn't forge
fifteenth-century printed books—although perhaps

they sometimes fudged them up out of bits and pieces found lying around. Nor was there any reason to suppose that the late Jacob Trechmann was other than an impeccably honest dealer—or none except in the odd fact that he had sold to Charles Gribble as a desirable forgery what had turned out only to be a forgery of that again. It occurred to Appleby that if poor Mr. Trechmann's death became in any degree celebrated—if it proved intractably or sensationally mysterious—people might even set about forging forgeries of Manallace forgeries for what might be called their associative value. Logically, there was no point at which the process need cease. Once take satisfaction in counterfeiting counterfeits and a sort of infinite regress of the things became possible at once.

Appleby put aside this idle speculation and made to enter the shop. As he did so, he noticed a small oblong of cardboard lying at his feet. He picked it up. It seemed to be out of a card-index, and written on it in a neat script he read:

> *K. Burger, Monumenta Germaniæ et*
> *Italiæ typographica, 1892.*

But this had been roughly struck out, and under it was written in pencil:

> *Sorry, working in B.M.*
> *Back at six o'clock. J.T.*

There was a drawing-pin with its point ineffectively askew through the 'M' of *Monumenta*. It seemed clear that Mr Trechmann, whether to-day or on an earlier occasion, had made a somewhat inefficient attempt to affix this notice to the door of his shop. It appeared, too, that the exigencies of his business had at times been sacrificed to the pleasures of research in the vast repository of learning near-by. He seemed an unlikely sort of person to get himself murdered. Robbery, of course, might well have been a motive, since the modesty of the dead man's premises probably by no means corresponded to the value of what they contained. Yet the thief—if there had been a thief—had at least shown no interest in the conspicuously exposed incunables of the late Professor Ludwig von Zinzendorf.

Appleby paused for a moment longer on the threshold. He was noticing—and with an almost guilty pleasure—that his pulse had quickened. Returning to this sort of thing—for his looking in, so to speak, on common metropolitan homicide was precisely that—carried just the excitement that such affairs had carried thirty years ago—when he had driven up to them not only with the rule of law to vindicate, but also with a career to make. But he paused, too, to recall something else. Trechmann was the person who had sold Charles Gribble the Meredith forgeries purporting to be by Geoffrey Manallace. But Jimmy Heffer, the man apparently under suspicion of killing Trechmann, had been the person associated with Sir Gabriel Gulliver in the curious affair of the false Astarte Oakes and her (as it seemed) entirely genuine Rembrandt. Here, one might say, were two stories, which were at present equally obscure and problematical. And the dead Jacob Trechmann looked as if he might be a link between them. . . . The shop-door wasn't locked. Appleby pushed it open.

And there was the body.

There was the body, with disorder all around it. But whether there was any connection between the fact of this disorder and the circumstance that Trechmann had a bullet through his head, Appleby saw no immediate means of telling. The little shop looked as if it was always untidy, so that even a reckless pillaging operation would make little difference to its appearance. There was a little counter almost invisible behind buttresses of books and beneath sheaves of prints and papers. There were a few chairs similarly encumbered. There were valuable-looking books behind steel grilles and equally valuable-looking books on open, rather dusty shelves. In the middle of the floor there was what looked at first like an elaborate infernal machine, but which turned out to be a clockwork model of the solar system. And there was a bust of Homer hazardously perched on a pedestal formed out of bound volumes of the Proceedings of the British Academy.

The body was seated in an old swivel chair, and slumped forward over rather a narrow desk. Trechmann had been an elderly man, shabbily dressed, and with a bald patch on the back of his head. It was very exactly through the centre of this that the bullet had gone. Some blood had flowed from the punctured scalp. But, on the whole, there wasn't much mess.

Appleby stepped forward. The sight of this nondescript person, so efficiently and ruthlessly despatched, oddly moved him—so that he found himself ignoring a constable who had stepped indignantly forward, not knowing him from Adam. The dead man's left arm hung limply down to the floor. The right arm was flexed on the desk, and the fingers had contracted on an open book, crumpling its title-page. Automatically Appleby deciphered the print beneath the nerveless hand:

> *Premiers Monuments*
> *de l'Imprimerie en France*
> *au XVe Siècle.*

It was difficult not to feel that the late Mr Trechmann's pursuits had been of a singularly harmless kind.

"Excuse me, sir—but might that be something Top Secret-like?"

The constable, who was very young, had somehow been apprised of the newcomer's importance. And he was putting his best foot forward.

Appleby looked again at the large clockwork toy.

"Top Secret?" he said.

"I think I've seen something of the sort in pictures, sir. Like it might be about a bomb, sir. A working model of an atom, you might say, with the neutrons and molecules and all moving like they should."

"Ah—I see." This appeared to Appleby a very intelligent conjecture. "As a matter of fact, it's something of the sort on a larger scale. That's the sun, and that's the earth, and these are the other planets. You'll see that they've all got their moons—except that this one, sixth from the centre, has rings."

"Saturn, sir?"

"I believe so. And the thing's called an orrery. Who's in charge here?"

"Inspector Parker, sir." The young constable nodded towards an inner door. "Through there, he is. And I'm waiting the word to get the body away. We've had the whole outfit now, sir—photographers and all. But now the Inspector is marking time, as you might say."

Appleby smiled.

"You mustn't criticize Inspector Parker, except to Inspector Parker. And do something about securing that outer door. We might have anybody walking in."

The constable did as he was told. Appleby went on into the inner room. It was much like the outer one, except that it was not furnished with a corpse. Inspector Parker, looking far from amiable, was standing at one end of it. At a hastily cleared square of table a uniformed sergeant was sitting over a blank notebook, visibly sweating at the effort of doing nothing at all. And in an ancient basket-chair in a corner, apparently engaged simply in giving Parker sour look for sour look, was a young man of wholesome appearance and athletic build.

"Mr Heffer?" Appleby asked, as his two subordinates got to their feet.

The young man didn't rise.

"Yes," he said. "Are you another policeman?"

"I am. And my name is Appleby."

"How do you do?" the young man said—civilly but entirely without interest.

"My wife, Mr Heffer, is much distressed that you were unable to dine with us."

"Oh, good Lord!" Now the young man did tumble

to his feet. "I say—what a frightful thing. But I did clean forget. Please explain to Lady Appleby. And of course I'll call and apologize just as soon as ever I can."

At this Inspector Parker, who had been obtrusively impassive before so startling an event as Appleby's appearance, spoke for the first time. It was briefly.

"Um," Inspector Parker said.

"And 'Um' to you," the young man said rather childishly. "Why can't you *do* something?" He turned to Appleby. "Why don't they arrest me, if they want to? This chap will do nothing but ask me to be reasonable—by which he seems to mean that I should pour my life history into the sergeant's waiting notebook. Why doesn't he caution me, and say I ought to send for a solicitor, and that sort of thing?"

"I imagine, Mr Heffer, that he feels there are circumstances of which you could give him a perfectly simple explanation if you were disposed to. As for your solicitor, I should certainly advise you to have him along. Summoning him will not establish the slightest adverse inference as to your position in this affair."

"I'll be damned if I summon anybody. And we've been staring at each other like this for hours, with the consequence that I've been extremely discourteous to your wife. And all because I happened to find old Trechmann shot dead. It's outrageous!"

"That a harmless man should be murdered?"

"Well, yes—that too, of course." Jimmy Heffer seemed a little checked by this.

"Then might it not be reasonable that we should approach the matter in a co-operative spirit?" Appleby turned to Inspector Parker. "Just what is the situation, Parker, and what do we want to know?"

"Well, sir, Mr Heffer has some story about an old woman."

Appleby frowned. He plainly thought poorly of this as the beginning of an expository speech.

"*Some story*, Parker? I don't think we can have that. It carries an implication of prevarication which isn't at all proper at this stage. I can see that Mr Heffer is an irritating person—or at least that he is behaving in an irritating manner now. But irritated is just what we mustn't get. So let's start again."

"Yes, Sir John. Well, the circumstances are these. At just after six o'clock this evening a constable on his beat turned into this street from the direction of the British Museum. He believes himself to have been aware of two persons, both male, walking down it in the same direction as himself, and a little ahead of him. Unfortunately, as it turns out, his attention was then distracted. He had occasion, that is to say, to examine the window of the stationer's and newsagent's shop near that end of the street."

Appleby considered this gravely.

"Wasn't that rather an idle occupation on this constable's part, Parker?"

"A matter of vigilance, sir. He had reason to suppose that the window might be displaying publications of a pornographical character."

"Well, well! And what was it that he failed to observe as a consequence of this distracting pornography?"

"He failed to observe what had happened to the two persons walking down the street in front of him. Not, of course, that there was any particular reason why he *should* observe them. But he is fairly sure that the street was empty when he heard a shot."

"Heard a shot? It was a deuced clever thing to hear, wasn't it, when walking in the direction of one of the most noisy thoroughfares in London? Do you mean he heard a bang which might have been any sort of bang?"

"No, sir." Inspector Parker was respectfully re-proachful. "This man happens to have received a good deal of instruction in small arms, and he knew at once that he had heard a revolver shot. He walked forward rapidly, and became aware of the open door of this shop. He paused, and there was a perceptible fume."

"A what?"

"A smell of gunpowder, sir, if one may speak very roughly. One can't fire a pistol without a bit of stink."

"True enough. And then?"

"He entered, and found Mr Heffer here."

"I see. And what was Mr Heffer doing?"

"According to the constable, sir, he was standing directly behind the dead man, with a revolver held in his right hand."

"And what was Mr Heffer doing according to Mr Heffer?"

"Just that, Sir John. There is no conflict of testimony at that particular point."

"That's something, I suppose." Appleby turned to the young man. "You confirm that, Mr Heffer?"

"Certainly I do. I'd picked up this revolver, or whatever it was. But I hadn't yet really looked at it. I was looking, you see, at the old woman. Or rather, at where the old woman had been."

"Or rather at *that*, all right," Parker said grimly. "For there was certainly no old woman when the constable entered the shop."

CHAPTER SIX

APPLEBY HAD LIT a pipe. He had tapped an open packet of cigarettes which the sweating sergeant had inefficiently failed to conceal—with the result that the sergeant, in a great awe, obediently took out a cigarette and lit it.

"Excellent," Appleby said. "Now we're really making progress. As only Mr Heffer saw the old woman, only Mr Heffer can tell us about her. Mr Heffer, go ahead."

"What's that?" Heffer had started—so that Appleby received the momentary impression that the young man hadn't been listening. Indeed, it was almost as if he had been listening for something else. "Oh, the old woman. Well, it was pretty queer."

"A number of things seem to me to be that, Mr Heffer. For instance, it isn't clear to me why we are all holding a sort of vigil in this not very comfortable shop."

"Entirely Mr Heffer's affair, sir," Parker interrupted. "I invited him to come to a police station and give his account of the matter there. But he refused to budge, unless put under arrest. And I have regarded that as—um—premature. So Mr Heffer has insisted, you may say, on staying put—and on being most uncommunicative as well."

"A sort of sit-down strike?"

"Well, at least a trial of patience, sir. But perhaps we are going to hear something now."

"Quite so—about this old woman. But first, Mr Heffer, could you put yourself to the trouble of telling us why you came into this shop at all?"

"Why I came in? Oh, just to look round."

"At just after six o'clock? You knew it would be open?"

"I just hadn't thought about it. I wasn't making a special journey, you know. Just passing."

"Where from, and where to?"

"Where from?" Again Heffer's attention appeared to have strayed. "I was coming from the B.M., where I'd been doing a bit of reading. And I was going back to my flat, to change and go out to dinner with your wife and yourself. Odd, isn't it? Here we are in quite a different relationship."

"Do you commonly spend your holidays in the B.M.?"

"Holidays?" Heffer was startled.

"I think it's a fact that, quite recently, you made rather an abrupt decision to begin a holiday due to you? But we might have a little conversation about that later. You came into this shop to look round. Had you ever done that before?"

"Dear me, yes. Often enough."

"I see. Well, was there anybody else in the street— anybody who might have entered the shop a minute before you?"

"I really can't say. I can't say, at all. I wasn't looking or thinking, you know."

"Did you hear a shot?"

"I'm terribly sorry, but I'm afraid I didn't. I can't have been listening either."

"Very well, Mr Heffer. You entered the shop. What then?"

"There was this old woman. She was standing looking at Trechmann, who had been shot through the back of the head."

"Did she look as if she might have done the shooting?"

"Not in the least. She had a bucket in one hand and a mop in the other."

"Was she agitated?"

"She certainly didn't seem to be. She turned to me as I came in and said: 'Shot 'im 'e 'as'." Heffer paused. "Do I make that intelligible? 'Shot him he has' was what was intended."

"Quite so. And then?"

"She said: 'Perlice work that is and no cleaning 'ere neither not till they're through'. And she turned and walked out of the shop and into this inner room. She wasn't seen again."

Inspector Parker could be heard breathing heavily. Appleby gave him a restraining glance and then turned again to the young man.

"You realize, Mr Heffer, that you are ascribing a somewhat improbable course of conduct to this old woman?"

"Well, it was certainly surprisingly phlegmatic. Perhaps she was feeble-minded. I hadn't time to think about it, you know, because the policeman came in from the street a moment later. You'll be able to settle the point when you find her."

"If we ever *do* find her," Parker said. "And if you ask——"

He broke off at a gesture from Appleby. From somewhere in the rear of the premises two sounds were
making themselves heard. One was a clanking. The
other could be described as a slip-slopping. Their
association could conjure up one image only. And this
was almost instantly vindicated. A door opened, and
there stood in it an old woman. She was wearing carpet
slippers, and she carried a pail, a mop, a broom, a con-
trivance for kneeling on, and a number of dusters. The
appearance of the four men revealed to her was something which she seemed to find wholly unsurprising.

"That there Mr Trechmann's corpus," the old
woman said, "would it 'av been taken to the mor-
guary?"

Parker's difficulty in the matter of respiration increased. Nor did he seem better pleased when Heffer,
without obtrusiveness, rose, tipped a pile of books and
papers from a chair, and invited the new arrival to sit
down.

"No," Appleby said. "Not yet. But it won't be long
now."

"I got to thorough through that there shop, I 'ave."
The old woman, who was plainly gratified by Heffer's
attention, had sat down composedly. "And 'uffkins my
name is. 'arriet 'uffkins. And Missus, although in a
widowed state."

"Mrs Huffkins," Appleby asked gravely, "will you
explain to us how you came to leave these premises
immediately after having come upon Mr Trechmann's
body?"

"Give it time to settle, was what I said to myself.
And I went to the pichers. Mark you, *'e* was 'ere."

Mrs Huffkins pointed a grubby finger at Heffer. "Gentleman, if ever I saw one, and well able to 'andle the perlice."

"So you felt," Appleby asked, "that you could leave it all to him, and you downed bucket and brooms and went off to the cinema? And now, at this late hour, you have simply returned to get on with your job?"

"That's it, mister. That's it in a coconut."

At this the sweating sergeant spoke for the first time. "Nutshell," he said. "That's what she means, sir. Nutshell. Not literate, she isn't."

"No doubt you are right, Sergeant." Appleby paused to get his pipe going again. "Mrs Huffkins, there is one point I must get quite clear. Could this gentleman —whose name is Mr Heffer—have shot Mr Trechmann, withdrawn from the shop, and then given the appearance of just having entered when you first saw him?"

"In course 'e couldn't." Mrs Huffkins answered as one who, whatever her intellectual limitations, would make a rock-like and impregnable witness. "It couldn't 'av 'appened—not in the time between when I 'eard the shot and saw what I saw. Besides, I saw 'im that done it, didn't I?"

"You *saw* 'im that done it?" Once more the sergeant was unable to refrain from interrupting. "You mean you saw 'im that done it a-doing of it, and then you walked out and went to the pictures? Inside, you ought to be."

"You mustn't make suggestions, Sergeant, as to where Mrs Huffkins ought, or ought not, to be." Appleby shook his head seriously. "Although her

behaviour, it has to be admitted, was not wholly that of
a responsible citizen. Mrs Huffkins, are we to understand that you actually saw Mr Trechmann being
shot?"

"I didn't say that, I didn't—and you can't put it on
me that I did. As I come in through this-'ere back shop,
there was Mr Trechmann with an 'ole in 'is 'ead.
And there was someone what 'ad dropped 'is gun on
'earing me, and was out through the other door—the
one to the little back stair—just as I came in and caught
a glimpse of 'is back. And then in come this gentleman
as anyone can see, Mr 'effer, from the street. So it's
none of my business now, I thinks, and I leaves 'im
to it."

There was a moment's silence. Inspector Parker
looked glum. He was seeing, clearly enough, that as
the killer of Jacob Trechmann young Mr Heffer
would never be worth a night's board and lodging in a
police cell. Heffer himself, who ought to have been
looking correspondingly relieved, was in fact paying
very little attention again. There was a strained look on
his face. And he was reaching into a pocket—Appleby
supposed it was to pull out a watch—when the thing
happened.

A bell rang. It rang in the room in which this queer
conference had been transacting itself. And it was
pretty obvious that it had been rung at the front door
of the shop. It was the door, Appleby remembered,
that he had instructed the constable to secure.
Presumably the constable would now answer this
summons.

But this didn't happen. Something extremely surprising happened instead. Jimmy Heffer rose and shouted—shouted with all the power of his athlete's well-developed lungs.

"Clear out! Run! Run like mad!"

The shout had rung out through the front shop, and clearly reached the ear it was intended for. It was followed by a moment's astounded silence, and then by a crash which sent Parker and the sergeant hurtling out of the room. Appleby followed. The front shop was precisely as it had been. The dead man sprawled as if in an elaborate demonstration of disregard. But the young constable was sprawling too. In too rapid a dash for the street door he had got entangled with the orrery —a good deal to that delicate contraption's detriment. He picked himself up as they watched, dashed to the door, fumbled at the lock, was out in the darkness of the street and running. The sergeant followed him. Appleby turned round to find Parker glaring at Jimmy Heffer in a condition of speechlessness. Mrs Huffkins was still in the inner room. Having been accommodated with a chair by a perfect gentleman, she was in no hurry to relinquish it.

"It would appear," Appleby said, "that we now have the explanation of Mr Heffer's sit-down strike." He turned to the young man. "Do you realize the extreme gravity of your action just now?"

"Gravity? Nonsense!" Heffer was blandly incredulous. "These people of yours have been bothering and badgering me for hours. And when that bell rang I jolly well thought they deserved to have their legs pulled."

"Are you seriously claiming, Mr Heffer, that you don't know who rang that bell?"

"Of course I don't. Probably it was a street urchin. But you all rose magnificently to my little joke."

This was more than Inspector Parker proved willing to take.

"I think you'll find," he said, "a magistrate rising magnificently to it too. I regret that I must——"

But at this Appleby interrupted.

"Just a moment, Parker. Here are your men back again. Empty-handed, I think." He turned to the young constable as he came puffing through the door. "No good?"

"I'm afraid not, sir. Hopeless, once you're round that corner. Plenty of people still on the street, and plenty of buses to nip on to."

"And you saw nothing?"

"Just a glimpse, sir, right at the start. Somebody taking the corner at the double."

"A street urchin, would you say?"

"Certainly not, sir. Long trousers, and carrying a parcel. That's all I could swear to."

"A man, in fact?"

"Well, sir, it might be or it might not. Plenty of women in slacks nowadays."

"Perfectly true." Appleby thought for a moment. "Parker," he said, "I think you'll find that Mr Heffer is now willing to make a statement of sorts. No doubt it will follow the general lines of our conversation. Get it down—and Mrs Huffkins's as well—and speak pretty sharply to somebody about not having collected that body. These proceedings have been grotesquely long drawn out, and wouldn't sound at all well in the Press. The sooner we are all in bed the better."

Parker was looking balefully at Heffer.

"But don't you think, sir——"

"No, Parker—frankly I don't. We can all begin thinking about this again in the morning—and it may well be that Mr Heffer will have to think hardest of all. But we can't, in my opinion, do anything more now."

And at this Jimmy Heffer lazily stretched his athletic body, so that Appleby thought what an odd type he was to be curating pictures.

"That's just what I've been thinking for some time," Heffer said. He made as if to yawn, and then checked himself. "I say," he said anxiously to Appleby, "you will explain to Lady Appleby, won't you? I do feel terribly bad about that."

"Mr Heffer, if you extricate yourself from this affair with nothing more than a broken dinner engagement to feel bad about I shall feel disposed to congratulate you."

"Oh, I say! I call that rather a narky remark. Perhaps my little joke just now wasn't in very good taste. Presence of death, and all that"—and at this Heffer gave a nod in the direction of Jacob Trechmann's body—"but you needn't hold it against me, all the same."

Appleby had been preparing to leave the shop. Now he came to a halt near the door.

"Mr Heffer, I think it may well be that you have been guilty of grave folly. But I do *not* think that you are what is known as a silly ass. Spare yourself the effort of trying to appear so."

Heffer was silent for a moment. He might have been considering how to take this.

"Sorry," he said. "You're quite right in a way. But if I've been behaving idiotically it's because this" —and again he nodded towards the body—"has been quite a shock to me. I've never run into it before— violent death, I mean. I was too young for the war, you know." He hesitated. "It makes one think."

"No doubt."

"Seeing—well, ruthlessness." Heffer had now brought himself, as with an effort, to look straight at the back of the dead man's head. "I mean, somebody has carried a job right through, haven't they? And there's always a sort of impressiveness in that."

CHAPTER SEVEN

APPLEBY CALLED ON Charles Gribble at nine o'clock next morning, and found the collector eating grilled kidneys while rather gloomily studying a sales catalogue.

"How did you hear about this fellow Trechmann's death?" Appleby asked. "The evening papers didn't have it."

"But the ten o'clock news did. I heard it on that and rang you up at once. Hope I didn't interrupt any conviviality."

Appleby shook his head.

"We had a dinner party, as a matter of fact. But some woman—Carl Bendixson's wife—began making faces at her husband rather early, so we'd just broken up. I went straight along to the scene of the crime." Appleby paused. "Would you describe yourself yesterday," he asked, "as having been out for Trechmann's blood?"

"My dear chap!" Gribble reached out for a coffee jug while at the same time staring at Appleby in consternation. "Are you suggesting that I may have put a bullet in the man because he sold me some dud manuscripts?"

"It would be very improper in me to suggest anything."

"If you ask me, it's very improper in you to come nosing round my breakfast-table. Cup of coffee?"

"No, thank you—although I take the offer as a forgiving one, all the same. And I'll say at once that the possibility that you plugged Trechmann in an access of indignation over your Manallace deal seems an exceedingly remote one. Still, you were intending to tackle the chap. Did you?"

"No—although I tried to. I went round by Bloomsbury, that's to say, on my way back to the City. But there was a notice on the door of his shop saying he wouldn't be back till six, because he was working in the B.M. I decided not to pursue him into the Manuscript Room or wherever, but to ring him up this morning and fix a meeting. As a matter of fact, I intended to ask him to lunch. Tactful approach, you know. I was dead keen to find out how he had come by those blasted forged forgeries. It looks as if I never shall, now."

"Possibly it does. By the way, between our parting yesterday afternoon and your hearing of Trechmann's death, did you tell anybody of the discovery of that fatal watermark on your supposed Manallace forgeries?"

"Certainly I didn't." Gribble was emphatic. "Nor have I—down to this moment. You and I are the only people in the world who know."

Appleby laughed.

"Well, one can't quite say that. Trechmann, or somebody from whom Trechmann had the stuff, may have known there was that little flaw in the faking."

Gribble nodded.

"I didn't mean that—although, mark you, my own conviction is that Trechmann was an honest enough dealer. I mean that only you knew of my sudden discovery of the horrid truth yesterday afternoon."

"Well, that isn't quite true, either. Don't you remember the chap who was pretending to be asleep?"

"Pretending to be asleep!" Gribble was highly indignant.

"Under a newspaper, you know. It's a turn people sometimes do put on in clubs, wouldn't you say, when they—um—don't want to be conversable? He left a little after we'd got it clear that you'd been cheated. You wouldn't have noticed who he was?"

"I haven't the slightest idea." Gribble seemed bewildered by Appleby's interest in the matter. "Perhaps one of the club servants might know. But it's a tricky thing to enquire about in a place like that. And could it possibly be important?"

"Possibly, yes. Probably, no. But this looks like being a thoroughly obscure affair, and I have to follow up everything I can."

"I can see that." Gribble absently reached for a square of toast. "But my little affair—and, after all, it *was* a little affair—didn't involve the sort of stakes that set people shooting each other." Gribble hesitated, and Appleby knew at once that he was struggling with his collector's discretion. *Silence is observed.*

"As a matter of fact," Gribble said, "I gave Trechmann £800 for those supposed Meredith forgeries by Manallace. If genuine—genuine Manallace, I mean— they'd have been, to my mind, cheap at a cool thousand. But nobody would murder anyone for a thousand pounds."

Appleby made no reply. In Stepney the amount is

round about a five-pound note. And a mother may get at least a crack on the jaw at a figure as low as half-a-crown.

"If Trechmann was shot because of something to do with fakes and forgeries," Gribble pursued, "it would have been a matter of larger stakes than any represented by the efforts of poor Geoffrey Manallace."

"Yes and no." Appleby was now prowling about Gribble's dining-room. He had to be careful not to bump into a number of rather costly objects. "Trouble over this paltry little eight-hundred-quid Manallace affair might have threatened some more general exposure." Appleby halted, stared through a window, and found that he was surveying Hyde Park. "At least that's how my mind inclines to work on the matter. What would have happened if you'd had the opportunity to tackle Trechmann? Let's begin with that. Of course it may be an utterly wrong approach. Your concerns with the fellow may be wholly irrelevant."

"Yes, I suppose they *may* be." Gribble now seemed reluctant to see himself thus possibly excluded from the case. "But, if that's so, it's a deuced odd coincidence, isn't it? A highly reputable dealer turns out either to have been tricked or to have been promoting trickery. And suddenly he's shot."

"Suppose Trechmann to have been in his shop yesterday afternoon. You'd have walked in. What would have happened then?"

"I'd have shown him that watermark, and pointed out that it was pretty well conclusive proof that the whole job wasn't by Manallace at all. And then I'd have said that, in the circumstances, I felt entitled to a full account of their provenance as he understood himself to have established it. That's to say, I'd have expected him to come clean. About that woman who had an influence over Geoffrey Manallace, and so forth."

"If Trechmann were honest, he would be bound to have a story which, if you were disposed to, you could follow up?"

"Certainly."

"Suppose him to be dishonest. If again you were pertinacious—and in the general interest of collectors you would probably feel bound to be so—sooner or later there would come a point at which his dishonesty would be exposed?"

"Undoubtedly. And that might be an occasion for the poor devil's blowing out his own brains. But scarcely for somebody else's stepping in and doing the job for him."

Appleby considered this.

"Once more, yes and no. If Trechmann were on the fringes of something really big, and if he was the sort of chap who might crack in a tight spot——"

"Yes, I see." Gribble was visibly impressed by his visitor's rapid professional dealing with the matter on hand. "But isn't it the simplest explanation—and therefore on the whole the likeliest—that Trechmann was shot in the course of robbery or attempted robbery? There must be a good deal of really valuable stuff tucked away in that shop."

"No doubt there is. But if common robbery was the motive, then the robber was of a very uncommon type. He didn't shoot because he was caught on the job. He walked in and killed a totally unsuspecting man as a

mere preliminary measure. Such things do sometimes
happen. A type of criminal exists whose ruthlessness
knows no bounds. But it is a comparatively rare type.
And I find it hard to associate with the kind of robbery
which could be brought off in Trechmann's shop.
Disposing of stolen property in the shape of *incunabula*
from the library of a German professor must be quite a
specialized affair. It scarcely seems a proposition that
would be attractive to a desperado."

"I can see all that," Gribble said. "So what?"

"Well, I remain interested in the Manallace affair,
for one thing. As I understand the matter, Trechmann
said to you, in effect: 'Here are some forgeries by
Geoffrey Manallace. I have satisfied myself that they
are really Manallace's work, but their provenance is a
matter of some delicacy.' Was that it?"

Gribble folded a table-napkin with precision.

"Just that," he said.

"Was there any suggestion that, if you had doubts
in the matter, he could provide further evidence?"

"Oh, certainly. The manuscripts had belonged to
this woman I was speaking of, who had been Manall-
lace's mistress. She was still alive, Trechmann said, and
at a pinch she could be appealed to. But the old soul
didn't much care for that sort of intrusion into her past,
and Trechmann hoped I'd take his word for it. And I
hadn't the slightest disposition not to do so. He's
always been entirely reliable, as I've said."

"But, since these forgeries are *not* by Manallace, it
is now clear that this story about a surviving mistress
must be moonshine?"

Gribble considered this for a moment.

"It certainly looks like that," he said. "But we can't be quite certain. I may have been deceived in Trechmann, and his whole story been a fib. But it is just possible that this woman really exists, and was herself unaware that her fakes were false. She might have bought them just as I was to buy them—believing they were her former lover's work."

"But wasn't it Trechmann's suggestion that they had been in this woman's possession from the start?"

"Well, yes—I think it was. But he may have picked up the facts rather inaccurately."

"Possibly so." Appleby didn't sound impressed. "By the way, Trechmann offered no clue as to who this woman was, or where she lived?"

"None at all. But if she has any real existence, and if she is still alive, she must be a very old woman now. Manallace, you remember, died nearly forty years ago."

"What about there being a hint of her in some biographical record? Have you looked up Manallace in *The Dictionary of National Biography*? Hasn't anybody written a life of him? Are no younger contemporaries who were really intimate with him still alive?"

"My dear Appleby, I'm not an absolute idiot." Gribble had shaken his head impatiently. "I haven't started collecting Manallace forgeries without trying to delve a little into the life of the man. And there's nobody in the record that I can think to identify with this lady. But that's not entirely surprising, after all. People kept much quieter about such affairs in those days than they do now. Mind you, I might try a little further research."

"I wish you would." Appleby had got to his feet.

"And now I'm off to take up the investigation elsewhere."

Gribble accompanied Appleby amiably to the door.

"Do you often," he asked curiously, "go sleuthing round like this nowadays?"

"Very seldom. It's my job to see that such matters are in competent hands, and if I push in myself there's likely to be the inference that I lack confidence in someone. But I'm risking that this time."

"The mystery appeals to you?"

"The mystery revolts me." Appleby snapped this out. "I don't know whether you've read of a lad in Stepney who has just killed somebody in circumstances of the most naked brutality? That's bad enough. But when I saw your little man Trechmann, shot dead through the back of the head, clearly without challenge or parley—well, I found myself liking it even less. As somebody said to me last night, it was a particularly ruthless sort of outrage. And I have a feeling that ruthlessness of that sort is catching. I propose to jump on it."

And opening the front door of his flat, Charles Gribble nodded soberly.

"Good hunting," he said. "I'm coming round to the view that Jacob Trechmann mayn't have been entirely what he seemed. But there was no call to do *that* to him."

CHAPTER EIGHT

RAIN FELL ON Bloomsbury, and the little street showed
forlorn and dismal. Opposite the premises of the late
Mr. Trechmann a press photographer lurked glumly in
a doorway on the off-chance of snapping some eminent
detective-officer from Scotland Yard. He glanced at
Appleby first hopefully and then incuriously. Appleby's,
clearly, wasn't a face he had in mind. Then some
memory must vaguely have stirred in him, for he
suddenly started into activity. But by this time the door
of the shop had been smartly opened from within, and
Appleby entered. It was the same young constable as
on the previous night. Although given this lonesome and
rather useless bit of care-taking he was a young man
determined to keep on his toes.

"Good morning," Appleby said. "I don't think I
got your name,"

"James, sir."

"Oh." Being engaged in looking rapidly round the
gloomy shop again, Appleby took this for a naïvely
familiar reply. "James what?"

The young constable blushed.

"Just James, sir. Henry James."

"I see." It would have been odder, Appleby thought,
if the young man had said "Joseph Conrad" or "Aldous
Huxley". He walked over to the desk across which
Trechmann's body had been sprawled. "Nothing been
happening here, I suppose?"

"Nothing at all, sir."

"Have our people taken anything away?"

"No, sir. Or only the weapon. There were more photographs being taken and inventories being made nearly all through the night. But I understand nothing has been disturbed."

"You can't have got much sleep. Why didn't you have them send you off duty this morning?"

"Well, sir, it's interesting, a case like this. Out of the ordinary, like."

"Quite so. Well, lock the door again, and turn on some lights." Appleby waited till this had been done. "Have you ever seen a stage farce, James? The good, clean English variety, of course."

"Well, yes, sir—I think I may say I have."

"Plenty of doors and windows, and people tumbling in and out on the dot. It was rather like that here last night, wouldn't you say?"

"Very much so, sir. Split second timing. But without a stage manager, so to speak. Just happening like that." It was evident that Constable James was delighted at being thus engaged in a discussion of the mystery. "And some of the cast too, sir, in a manner of speaking. That odd old woman, for instance. Walking in on a murder, and then walking straight out and going to the pictures. Like a play, that is. Not natural, at all."

"You regard Mrs Huffkins's conduct with suspicion?"

"Well, no, sir. That's the funny thing. You do get people behaving more like a play than the people who write plays would ever venture on. And that's Mrs

Huffkins, if you ask me. It's the young gentleman—Heffer the name was, wasn't it?—that I've been thinking on."

"Have you, indeed? Well, go on thinking, James—about Heffer and anything else. And if anything you think might be useful comes into your head, mention it to me at once. And now I'm going to have a look round on my own."

"Yes, sir. Thank you, sir." And Henry James retired to a corner of the shop, sat down, and knitted his brows. He was an ambitious youth, and disposed to take his instructions very seriously.

There were certainly plenty of doors. Two led from the front shop to the back, and a third from the front shop to a narrow corridor leading to a narrow staircase. From both the back shop and the corridor one could make one's way through different doors to a small enclosed yard at the back of the building, and from this again there was an exit to a dingy and more or less deserted cul-de-sac, curiously remote in feeling from the bustle of traffic which could be heard beyond it, from which the outer world could be gained through a low broad archway at one end. There was nothing much to be seen here except a row of garbage bins and three or four melancholy urban cats.

Appleby turned back into the shop and made a cursory examination of the stock. His impression was that Jacob Trechmann had operated only in a middling-large way, but that he had done so on a number of fronts. If you had gone into his establishment and expressed disinterest in the face of Professor von Zinzen-

dorf's volumes from the first cradles of printing, Mr
Trechmann would have been in a position to ask you
whether you would care to buy a few drawings by
Francesco Cossa or Baldassare Franceschini. If that in
turn had elicited no response, he might—had he
trusted the look of you—have conducted you to a
small strong-room rather notably well-stocked with
erotica and *curiosa*. The constable who had been so
laudibly vigilant in the matter of possible pornography in the local news-agent's would have found an
altogether higher class of article here. Appleby edified
himself with a quick glance through some of this—he
wondered whether Henry James had done the same—
and then moved on.

Presently it was occurring to him that the disorderly
manner in which Trechmann's business was conducted
was in fact a matter more of appearance than reality.
The random way in which things lay about or piled
themselves up was perhaps no more than a trick of the
trade. Conceivably it conveyed to innocent collectors
the impression that any sort of treasure might be found
lurking in the litter, and that the proprietor owned a
constitutional carelessness in material matters which
in favouring circumstances might be happily exploited
by a shrewd purchaser. Certainly the stock and all
recent transactions were carefully indexed in a filing
cabinet. It had been on one of these cards which
was for some reason no longer needed—that recording
the *Monumenta Germaniæ et Italiæ typographica*—that
Trechmann had scribbled his message about working
in the British Museum. Now it occurred to Appleby to
turn up the name of Manallace. And he found:

> *MANALLACE, Geoffrey (English scholar
> and forger, 1853-1922); manuscripts
> purporting to be by George Meredith
> (English novelist and poet, 1828-1909).*
> *Privately purchased.*

It seemed impeccably respectable. On the bottom of
the card there had been added in pencil a date and the
note:

> *Charles Gribble Esqre.* £500.

Appleby smiled grimly. He wasn't puzzled by the sum
of money recorded. Gribble had been asked to write
one cheque for £500 and another for £300. And
Gribble had not thought it incumbent upon him to ask
why. If Trechmann fiddled his tax-returns that was
Trechmann's affair.

Neither the front nor the back shop yielded any
further matter of interest, and Appleby thought he
would try upstairs. The upper regions had also been
Trechmann's, and they consisted of room after room—
none of them very large—crammed with books. There
was an enormous amount of eighteenth-century theo-
logy of the controversial order. The calf bindings of
these works were probably a good deal harder-wearing
than their arguments. And that, of course, was why
they were here. As long as there is money to be made in
England there will be gentlemen in need of making
too. And English gentlemen—even if of the variety
apt to establish a private bar and bar-tender in their
wives' drawing-rooms—must be equipped with ancient-
looking libraries. So good calf is never a drug on the
market.

But criminology rather than sociology is my business, Appleby thought—and moved up to the next storey. Here one turned out to be back with the fine arts again. But not so much with Baldassare Franceschini and that crowd as with more modern masters. There was a large body of biographical material here which looked as if it might be a private collection of Trechmann's own rather than destined for piecemeal sale. Appleby mulled around this for some time, although the stuff was more up Judith's street than his own. There was a privately printed volume of reminiscences of Sickert, Steer, Tonks, George Moore and their circle that he knew his wife had always wanted to get hold of. There was a similarly privately printed book about Utrillo and his mother. There was a collection of familiar impressions of Gauguin that it would have interested him to sit down and read himself. And so on. But he wasn't here fossicking for junk. He went up one higher still.

But here there were only attics. And these, except for some broken furniture and stacks of mouldering periodicals not fit to pulp, were empty and thick with undisturbed dust. So that was that.

Only it wasn't quite true that the dust was totally undisturbed. It didn't hold of the single narrow passage which led from the head of the stairs. Here footprints were discernible. They belonged, almost certainly, to the police who must have raked through the whole place on the previous night. Appleby followed them, all the same. They ended before a blank wall. But up the wall climbed a fixed iron ladder. There was raw plaster where it had been clamped to the wall. It hadn't been in position very long.

Appleby looked up at the trapdoor before which it ended. The fall of the roof was such that he saw this could scarcely give upon a further enclosed space accommodating a cistern or the like. It must take you out on the leads. And that was sensible enough. There was a very real risk of fire in an old place like this. And if fire broke out when you were high up in the building, it might well be that your best line of retreat would be to get up yet higher and escape by an adjacent building. Anyway—Appleby told himself—always go on till you're stopped. He put a foot on the lowest rung and went on.

The trapdoor was bolted from the inside. That was only prudent, if any precautions against burglary were to be taken at all. He pushed back the bolt. It moved very easily. He pushed up the trapdoor. That moved very easily too. And from the narrow ledges upon which its perimeter rested no dust fell. Not uninstructed by all this, Appleby mounted higher and shoved his head into open air. It was raining hard. But that couldn't be helped.

He was in a sort of broad lead gutter between sloping roofs. Water gurgled merrily over his shoes in a little river which seemed to run contentedly the whole length of the street. Nowhere were there any attic windows opening inwards upon this long tiled valley. Only here and there were chimney-stacks. And at more or less regular intervals—raised a foot above the level of the gutter to avoid flooding—were trapdoors similar to the one through which he had emerged. No doubt they would all be bolted too. If he were really a fugitive from some ghastly conflagration, he would presumably have to cool—and wet—his heels up here until somebody came along and rescued him.

But, of course, there was a job to do—and for a moment he thought half-heartedly of summoning Constable Henry James to do it. But he himself was already rather wet, and Henry James was presumably still thinking. So he might as well carry on himself. He advanced to the next trapdoor and tried to lift it.

Of course it wouldn't budge. As one might expect, it was secured from below. He moved on and tried the next. At least there was nobody who could possibly detect him in this odd procedure. This one was immovable also. He went on and tried a third. And up it came.

At this he had to pause and take thought. Being the most law-abiding of policemen, he might have paused and taken thought for longer, if only the rain hadn't now been getting down his neck. There was a perfectly good ladder at his feet—although, unlike the one by which he had ascended, it was of a sloping wooden sort, approximating to a rudimentary staircase. He climbed down, and let the trapdoor close above him.

He saw at once that this building—three along from Trechmann's—had in some way been remodelled so far as its interior went. Its roof-line was uniform with those on either side of it—hence his unimpeded progress along the gutter. But he was now standing in a single attic room which was both loftier and larger than any of Trechmann's. It was quite empty, and it lay in a clear cold light from one big northward-facing window. In one corner a space had been partitioned off. He crossed over to this, and found himself in one of those small indeterminate apartments, dubiously hovering between bathroom and kitchen, and with an unappealing lavatory beyond, which in London entitles a set-up of this sort to describe itself as a self-contained flat. He crossed to the only other door and found that it gave directly upon a staircase leading down to the next floor. There was nothing else up here. This big room and its adjacent chopped-off hutches occupied the whole area of the building.

The emptiness of the place was almost unnatural. There wasn't a wisp of straw, a match-end, a cigarette-butt negligently cast aside by the last removal-man who had bundled the last tenant's last possessions out of the place. There was nothing at all. Or there was only a smell.

And at least there was no mystery about *that*. Appleby had sufficiently moved about in his wife's world to recognize it instantly. A painter had, comparatively recently, occupied this studio flat.

But if this was no very startling detective deduction, neither was it, in all probability, a fact of the slightest relevance for Appleby's present enquiries. The amount of cubic space devoted in London to the lower reaches of artistic endeavour is—he was accustomed to say— one of the most depressing statistical facts that the metropolis afforded. And artists, moreover, are an impermanent and drifting community—perpetually deciding that this or that place is no good, and moving on to another. In London the number of studios of this

kind that were vacated daily must be quite considerable. And he was himself in this one now only as a
consequence of detective investigation that had degen-
erated into idle curiosity.

All the same, he decided not to go back as he had
come. So he took one more barren prowl round this
swept and voided space. And then he opened the door
and walked downstairs.

But he hadn't gone down half-a-dozen steps before
he halted in perplexity. He *had* seen something signifi-
cant. Or rather he had seen something that remotely
stirred a memory, but which he couldn't now place for
the life of him. He climbed up again—and then realized
that, as he had drawn the door of the studio to behind
him, he could enter it again only by the roof as before.
This was tiresome. And he was about to turn away
when he became aware that, to fulfil his present object,
he didn't have to re-enter the studio at all. For what
had pricked at his memory was something stuck in the
outside of the door. And it was nothing more than a
drawing-pin.

He levered it out, examined it closely, and stowed it
away in a match-box. Then he looked carefully at the
door. Perhaps because everything was rather damp up
here, the vanished object which the drawing-pin had
pierced had left on the paint an oblong impression so
precise that it could be accurately measured. Producing
a pocket-rule, Appleby accurately measured it. And
then he turned and went downstairs again.

It wasn't, as in Trechmann's place, the sort of staircase that went down through the body of the building.
Here, too, there had been some alterations, and this

was now an enclosed outer staircase off which doors opened on several small landings. On the ground floor there was no doubt a shop. But the rest of the property had been converted into flats. And there didn't seem to be much life about them. He met nobody. He didn't hear a sound. You could do a lot of coming and going here without attracting notice.

And the entrance was at the back. This wasn't unexpected. The frontage on the street would be valuable as shop-space. So access to the flats had been arranged from that cul-de-sac at the rear which Appleby had already inspected.

There was again nobody about. There were only the cats and the garbage bins. Turning up his coat-collar— for it was again raining hard—Appleby began to make his way back to the late Mr Trechmann's yard. And then—once again—he stopped. Precisely the same thing had happened. It came, he supposed, of being out of training at this game. He had seen *something*. But what?

He retraced his steps. A dog had joined the cats, and was investigating one of the garbage bins with vigour. And that, of course, was it. Most of the bins were overflowing and with their lids askew. There were a couple like that at the bottom of a service hoist beside the flats. But there was a third . . .

Yes—on this one the lid was fitting snugly. And when he lifted it the bin was empty. More than that, it was *unnaturally* empty. Just as that flat had been *unnaturally* empty. No dustman had ever coped thus with such a receptacle since dustmen first began.

The spectacle—he was to reflect afterwards—must have been an odd one: a dampish person, formally dressed and carrying a certain professional authority, competing with a dog and a number of cats in the hopeful inspection of these humble but necessary utensils. And now he tilted the thing over to get a better light in its interior. He saw that it wasn't absolutely empty, after all. An irregular scrap of white paper—no more than an inch square—adhered to the bottom of the bin. He reached in, fished this out, and turned it over. He was looking at a representation of a human eye. More than this—he was looking at a *familiar* representation of a human eye.

It didn't make sense. Or, at least, at first it didn't do so. The eye wasn't even a whole eye, but only part of one. What there was of it was in colour—very much in colour. For a moment Appleby supposed that it might be from the cover of a magazine. But no pin-up girl ever had that eye. Nor was it likely that an eye from such a source would strike him with this mysterious sense of familiarity.

On second thoughts, there was only one explanation of it. What he had found was a scrap torn from a coloured reproduction of some painting with which he was acquainted. One more square inch, and he would probably be able to identify it. Once more he looked carefully in the bin—and carefully over the whole area round it. But a second square inch wasn't there. Of course—he reflected, as he made his way back to

Trechmann's shop—an expert would probably know. Gulliver would know. He'd ask Gulliver.

"Sir Gabriel Gulliver, sir."

Henry James, pale with excitement, had got this out on top of something incoherent that Appleby hadn't caught.

"Gulliver?" Appleby was shaking the rain from his overcoat. "What about him, man?"

"A telephone message from the Yard, sir. In his private office at the gallery. And would you go at once."

Appleby stared in dawning comprehension.

"You mean——?"

"Dead, sir. Shot through the back of the head."

CHAPTER NINE

At the top of the broad shallow steps, sheltered from the rain by the great portico, Inspector Parker stood with an elaborate air of negligence. When Appleby approached, he turned and walked ahead. Parker was much given to such harmless manoeuvres. At the moment, he was busy not attracting the attention of the Press—supposing the Press to be about. Gulliver's death—if it really was his death—had presumably not yet been made public.

People were buying catalogues, post-cards, colour-prints. People were giving up umbrellas and macin-toshes. A mob of school-children were being issued with little camp-stools which they would presently trail in the wake of a peripatetic lecturer. Meanwhile, they were staring in awe at the vast expanses of marble around them—all except one small and clearly obnox-ious boy with spots. He had discovered that the marble was merely painted on, and he was drawing the attention of a companion to this satisfactory discovery. In recesses of the building beyond these, and upon benches very comfortably upholstered at the cost of the nation, sundry citizens dozed, cuddled, toiled at cross-word-puzzles or lunched off slabs of chocolate and bananas. Parker, ignoring all this artistic fervour, led the way down into a kind of splendiferous and gigantic basement.

"Dead?" Appleby asked, when he judged that a sufficient degree of seclusion had been attained.

"Oh, yes—oh, dear me, yes." Parker spoke with gloomy satisfaction. "Instantaneous. Absolutely instantaneous. And precisely as last night, you know. Bang through the back of the head as he sat at his desk."

"But I don't think Gulliver had the same bald patch. So not precisely the same sort of target."

"Well, no." Parker seemed doubtful whether to consider this reservation on Appleby's part frivolous. "But two identical crimes like this aren't comfortable, sir. Not within something like twelve hours of each other. And one of the victims a person of eminence. It scares people, a thing like this. Maniac at large, and so on. One more big-wig, and we'll have half the big-wigs of London ringing up to say that they won't positively object to being given police protection. Thank goodness that little chap Trechmann wasn't a big-wig too."

"Quite so." Appleby, although not much worried by the bigness or littleness of wigs, sympathized with Parker. At the same time, this didn't dissuade him from a mild pulling of his colleague's leg. "And our friend Heffer?" he asked. "I suppose he was found standing behind the body?"

"Certainly, Sir John. Just that."

For a moment Appleby supposed that Parker too had given way to frivolity. But this was clearly impossible.

"My dear man," he murmured, "let's get this absurd affair cleared up rather quickly."

"Yes, sir. You express my own feeling exactly. This way, sir."

There was at least a considerable contrast in the settings of the Trechmann and Gulliver fatalities. Sir Gabriel had died in an enormous and cavernous room like a mausoleum. One end was taken up by tall windows which proved to be only of the slightly subterraneous order. The other was occupied by a vast historical painting by John Martin. It was called The Destruction of Carthage and depicted a huge harbour crowded with grappling vessels, surrounded by colossal moles crammed with improbable pylons, cenotaphs and fortifications, garnished with three or four hundred drowned, stabbed, crushed or dismembered human bodies, and illumined throughout by a lavish display of fireworks diversified by skyward-roaring flames. All this now made a kind of backcloth to one additional corpse, that of the late Director of this imposing institution.

And he had been a queer chap—Appleby thought, looking down at him dispassionately. What quirk of character, for instance, had drawn a man whose business was with Botticelli and Rembrandt to live with a monstrosity like that? Appleby turned back to the painting. Not, he thought, that John Martin didn't have his points. There had at least been a kind of honest ruthlessness to give dignity to that second-rate imagination.

"Plenty of doors here, too," Appleby said. "These little incidents do seem to transact themselves in efficient theatrical settings. That was a secretary's room we came through?"

Parker nodded.

"Yes—and she was there all the time. A Miss Quinn. It was a great shock to her. We haven't revived her yet."

"Haven't revived her! What on earth do you mean?"

"Only that she did rather an obstinate faint—or perhaps hysterical turn. She's in a room along the corridor, with a doctor who says she must be taken slowly."

"Well, well. And those two doors on the other side of this great barn of a room?"

"That one"—Parker pointed—"leads to Heffer's room, just across a passage."

"Ah, yes—where the Rembrandt was inspected."

"The Rembrandt, sir?" Parker was puzzled.

"Just something that came into my head. Probably with no relevance at all. And that other door?"

"It takes you into a small room where Gulliver kept some clothes. Then there's his wash-place, and then a corridor again. Not much used. Anybody could have come and gone that way, quite unobserved."

"But not without knowing the building? I mean, there are no notices and arrows and things, saying 'This way to the Director'?"

"No, sir. Of course there's nothing like that. A person would have to have information. But it wouldn't be terribly hard to come by."

"Quite so. Parker—have you ever thought how easy it is to kill people?"

"Well—yes, sir. It's our business, I suppose, to reflect along those lines from time to time. And yet there isn't a great deal of killing done. Broadly speaking, the disposition must be absent in the vast majority of the population. It's an encouraging thought."

"No doubt." Appleby took a turn about the room. "Where's Heffer?"

"In his own room. There are a couple of constables keeping an eye on him."

"But no doctor? Heffer didn't put on a fainting fit like this sensitive Miss Quinn?"

"As a matter of fact, I rather gather that he did. Or the next thing to it. And I've seen myself that he's very much upset."

"Not the sort of cool-customer turn that he put over last night?"

"Very far from it. Really shaken." Parker hesitated. "You'll agree, sir, that when one catches the killer after an affair like this, he's often disconcertingly remote from his deed. Impassive or calmly negative. But it isn't always so. I've seem them trembling as this man Heffer has been trembling."

"He might well tremble—forming the habits he seems to have been doing. Whose body will he be found posed behind tomorrow? It may be yours or mine, my dear Parker."

"Of course there are professional risks." Parker offered this generalization in a finely wooden way. "But they're not things that you'd expect *him* to hit up with." And he jerked a thumb in the direction of the body. "Or that little fellow in Bloomsbury, either."

"I hope soon to be in a position to disagree with you there. And now you'd better tell me what's known, so far, about Round Two."

"I suppose it *is* Round Two?" Parker was cautious. "Of course, the manner of killing is a link. And so is Heffer."

"And so is the general context of both affairs."
Appleby was looking at John Martin's gigantic mas-
sacre again. "Art and literature and acquisitiveness.
But mostly, of course, acquisitiveness. Now, go ahead."

"Eleven a.m., sir. Sir Gabriel Gulliver sitting alone
in this room, presumably as we see him now. Across the
corridor, Mr. Heffer alone in *his* room."

"Ah." Appleby nodded. He had sat down and
lighted a cigarette—somewhat doubtfully, perhaps, on
account both of the body and of its impressive sur-
roundings. "So our young friend had regarded last
night's excitements as the climax of his holiday, and had
clocked in to work again?"

"Seemingly so, sir. And Miss Quinn was in *her*
room—the outer one we came through—doing some
typing. Any visitor for the Director in a regular way
would, of course, have been filtered past her after
signing a book in the head porter's office."

"A formal business, apparently. I had an idea that
Gulliver ran the place rather easily."

"I gather, sir, that all these museums and such-like
more or less follow government office rules. But, of
course, nobody *did* sign. There were no visitors,
whether by appointment or otherwise, for the Director
this morning."

"*Pallida Mors.*"

"Yes, sir—I grant you that." Parker was plainly
pleased by this reliance upon his Latinity. "In the
midst of life we are in death, as another ancient
authority has it. But Sir Gabriel, no doubt, was thinking of other matters. About buying another picture for

the place—or whether he would have a glass of claret with his lunch." Parker paused only briefly on this flight of fancy. "Then somebody walked in on him, shot him dead, and walked out again. Either Heffer, operating from his own room, or an unknown, operating through the little anteroom and from the corridor beyond the wash-place."

"But if it was Heffer—and we seem to have had something like this discussion before—then he *didn't* walk out again. Because he was actually found here with the body."

"Yes, sir. But the body has a bullet in it. And Heffer had no weapon. This room concealed no weapon. Indeed, we're already almost certain that no weapon is concealed anywhere that Heffer could possibly have reached in the time available to him."

"How much time?"

"Well, sir, it seems to have been like this. The corridor between this room and Heffer's takes a right-angled turn, so that it runs just behind *that*." Here Parker pointed at John Martin's canvas. "Round that corner, so that they couldn't see whether anything was happening or not happening between this room and Heffer's, three employees of the place were working just on eleven o'clock. I gather they were preparing to get a large picture up through a trapdoor into a main gallery. And they heard a shot."

"They knew it to be a shot?"

"Yes and no. Unfortunately they paused to argue about it. One of them thought it might be a picture falling. That, no doubt, is felt to be the utmost possible disaster in a concern like this. Then they decided it *had* been a shot. So they ran down the corridor and made that right-angled turn. That meant that a blank wall was in front of them, this room on their right, and Heffer's room on their left. They went for Heffer's room. Perhaps that was less alarming than charging in on the Director. They knocked, got no reply, went in, and found the room empty. They repeated the process with *this* room—and found Gulliver's body precisely as you see it now, and with Heffer standing beside it."

"Heffer might have shot Gulliver, nipped through that other door into the anteroom, handed over the weapon to a confederate who made off with it, and then himself immediately have returned to the seat of his crime. It sounds as if there might have been time enough for that."

"Yes, sir. I agree. But it's hard to see that there would have been any sense in such a plan."

"I rather concur. But what about this Miss Quinn?"

"As I think I've said, there can be no doubt that she was in her own room—the room commanding the regular entrance to this one—during the whole material time. She was found there—either screaming, or fainting, or both—when it eventually occurred to someone to go in and look for her. There had been the usual sort of confusion, of course, that you get on top of an affair like this. Perhaps you'd like to tackle the young woman yourself?"

Appleby considered for a moment.

"Yes," he said. "We'll go along and talk to her— that doctor you spoke of permitting."

Miss Quinn proved to be an abundant young person,

whose charms were doubtless at their most striking when set off by a heaving bosom and a distraught air. The doctor who had been called in, and who had gone on to attend to the lady after pronouncing Gulliver to be indubitably dead, was just leaving her when Appleby and Parker arrived. He expressed himself dryly to the effect that her condition was scarcely serious. But if her reaction to the mere hearing of a pistol-shot, he added, appeared to be altogether excessive, it would be unwise to conclude that she actually knew more than she was disposed to tell. On such occasions it was to be observed that genuine shock and the most tiresome play-acting regularly got themselves mixed up, and it was a waste of time trying to distinguish the one from the other.

Appleby felt that, medically speaking, this was no doubt true. Legally, however, it might be another matter. And he introduced himself to Miss Quinn without much ceremony. She was being attended by a motherly person who had been summoned from the ladies' cloak-room for the purpose, but who remained silent during the interview except for occasionally contributing a heavy sigh.

"I understand, Miss Quinn, that at the time of——"

Miss Quinn's bosom heaved. It was rather as if she had been squeezed elsewhere, and as if this necessary pneumatic consequence had followed.

"I am much to blame," Miss Quinn said. Her voice contrived to be at once strong and tremulous. "I am very much to blame."

"Why do you say that?"

"I condoned it," Miss Quinn said. She sighed—and

at once the female attendant sighed too. "For long I condoned it. The natural weakness of a woman. How bitterly I regret it now."

Inspector Parker breathed so heavily that Appleby was afraid he might begin to sigh as well. He contended himself, however, with producing a notebook in ominous silence.

"May I ask," Appleby said, "just what you condoned, Miss Quinn?"

"The women."

"Ah—the women." Appleby paused to consider this. "I suppose you must mean women who might be described as women in Sir Gabriel's life?"

"Exactly," Miss Quinn said.

"I am not sure that you mayn't be imagining things. But, even supposing that these women existed, how can you be said to have condoned the matter? It had nothing to do with you, and you bore no responsibility."

"They came here."

"You are referring merely to the fact that ladies visited the Director in his office? As it happens, my wife occasionally did so."

"Ah—Lady Appleby." And Miss Quinn nodded in a fashion that, although theatrical, did suggest that she wasn't entirely lost in a world of prurient fantasy. "But she comes in the proper way—which is through my room."

"You mean that Sir Gabriel was in the habit of receiving ladies who came in by the back way?"

"Yes. As he did this morning. I heard——"

"One moment, Miss Quinn. Did male visitors sometimes come in by that way too?"

"Well, yes. Some did."

"Visitors who ask for the Director, even for the purpose of making a social call, sign a book, and wait while a message goes through to you, and so forth?"

"Yes."

"Wouldn't it be reasonable, then, for Sir Gabriel to mention to intimate friends that they were always welcome to drop in on him by this less formal route?"

"Not all those women."

The motherly person gave her heaviest sigh yet. She appeared to take the darkest view of the whole situation.

"Come, Miss Quinn. We must be thoroughly sensible in a matter of this kind. Sir Gabriel liked the company of women, no doubt. But do you seriously suggest that there was something clandestine and improper in the visits you have in mind—visits taking place in a room into which, I imagine, you were entitled to enter at any time with business that required his attention?"

"You should have heard what was going on this morning," Miss Quinn said.

The motherly woman, in addition to a sigh, contrived a shocked noise with her tongue. Parker opened the notebook and brought out his fountain-pen. Unless Miss Quinn were to be judged as living in a world of mere day-dream, something was going to emerge at last.

"It is, of course, fortunate that *you* heard it," Appleby said. "Please tell us about it now."

"Passion," Miss Quinn said. She looked round, and appeared dissatisfied with the effect she had produced. "Guilty passion," she said.

"Come, Miss Quinn. I think your imagination may be running away with you. Let us say that a lady came to see Sir Gabriel this morning. At what time?"

"Ten to eleven. I looked at my watch."

"Thank you. And within a few minutes of eleven o'clock Sir Gabriel was dead. So what is this talk of guilty passion, please?"

"Well—they were excited. I could hear that. It wasn't just social talk."

"As Sir Gabriel was presently shot, that seems very likely. But it is something rather less specific than you have been suggesting, you know. You didn't recognize the woman's voice?"

"No."

"Had you heard it before, would you have been aware of the fact? Was it distinct enough for that?"

Miss Quinn shook her head. She appeared discouraged.

"I wouldn't have known," she said. "And I couldn't make out a word. But there was a quarrel."

"A quarrel? Are you sure?"

"Well, a dispute."

"You are sure of *that*?"

"An argument. But at the end Sir Gabriel was certainly angry. He raised his voice."

"So that you could hear what he said?"

"Yes." Miss Quinn hesitated. "Because by that time I had——" She hesitated again. "Well, by that time, I had gone to listen—just a little."

"I see. And what was it that you heard Sir Gabriel say in this raised voice?"

"That he would have nothing to do with it."

Appleby stared in astonishment.

"My dear young lady—do you realize that you may have to give evidence in a criminal trial? And be required to talk sense? Does this remark which you overheard seem to have anything to do with what you call guilty passion?"

"Well, no. But it was the whole tone of the thing."

"Never mind the whole tone of the thing. Did you manage to distinguish any other words whatever?"

"Yes. Only a minute later, when Sir Gabriel spoke in a loud angry way again. He said that he would make the communication at once."

Parker raised his pen.

" 'Make the communication at once,' Miss Quinn?"

"Yes."

"Thank you." Parker wrote gravely. "And then?"

"And then there was the shot."

Parker continued to write.

"And *then*?" Appleby asked.

"And then?" As if at the recollection of strong emotion, Miss Quinn's bosom again dangerously heaved. "And then," she said luxuriously, "I swooned away."

There was a moment's silence while Parker's pen still moved.

" 'Swooned away,' " Parker said impassively—and shut his notebook.

CHAPTER TEN

"And now," Parker said grimly, "we'd better see Mr Heffer."

"Certainly." And Appleby nodded. "In fact, we'd better catch him before he goes out to lunch."

"Goes out to lunch!" Parker was scandalized. "Good Lord, sir! You don't suggest that after two occasions on which——"

"It's no good, Parker. You can't hold him. To last night's affair, you'll agree, there is only one material witness—Mrs Huffkins. And Mrs Huffkins lets Heffer right out. Of course her own conduct was so extraordinary and seemingly irresponsible that she would have a rough time in the box. But there she is. As for this morning, there's again no more than a single material witness. Of course this Quinn girl may be a confederate of Heffer's, and the female visitor have no real existence. But the present presumption has to be that Miss Quinn is more or less speaking the truth as she sees it. She hasn't a very nice mind, perhaps, but I doubt whether she's a deep deceiver. And her story—together, of course, with the absence of all trace of a weapon—lets Heffer out almost as definitely as Mrs Huffkins's story does. We'll only embarrass the investigation at the present stage by arresting or trying to detain young Heffer. He must be kept an eye on, of course. That's a different matter. And now we'd better go and be civil to him."

"Civil to him!" Parker's indignation was enhanced. "Do you remember that shout he gave last night, sir? Even if it was a joke—which it certainly was not—it could be made the subject of a charge perfectly adequate to hold him on."

"No doubt. But he may have a more interesting career, from our point of view, if *not* held."

"Well, sir—that's a different matter." Much mollified, Parker marched down a corridor and threw open a door. "The Commissioner," he said impressively.

Two constables sprang to their feet. And so too, this time, did Jimmy Heffer.

But it wasn't out of politeness. Appleby took one glance at the young man and recognized somebody to whom something had happened—something so shattering as to blot out all consideration of manners whether good or bad. Heffer had sprung up like a man whose simple instinct is to get his back to a wall and defend himself.

"Good morning, Heffer." And Appleby gave a brisk neutral nod. "You and I do meet in the most extraordinary circumstances, do we not? If only you had managed to come to dinner last night we might be on very much more familiar terms."

"Let me say at once that I have nothing to say to you."

"Then you are unlike Gulliver's secretary. She has been saying quite a lot."

"Hysterical gibberish. If you listen to that girl, the more fools you." Heffer had flashed this out.

"I would agree with you about the hysteria—or a

certain element of it. On the gibberish I am not so sure." Appleby paused. "Would you agree with her, by the way, that Gulliver put in a good deal of time chattering to women in his room?"

Heffer, who was now literally standing with his back to a wall, made an odd movement of recoil which brought him hard up against it.

"I say again that I have nothing to say to you. Twice within twenty-four hours I find myself standing beside a murdered man. And you arrive and ask me idle questions. Why not *act*? Arrest me, charge me, put me on trial. I haven't killed anybody, but you have a sporting chance of convincing a jury that I have. And it's your *only* chance, it seems to me. Because it's evident to me that neither you yourself, nor this man Parker, nor any of your understrappers, has a clue. Not a clue."

If these provocative remarks were in fact designed to provoke action—and they seemed to have no other function—they singularly failed. Parker and the constables seemed instantly to turn to wood. And Appleby looked entirely amiable.

"I wonder," he said, "if you'd care to come out to lunch with me?"

If Heffer could have retreated another six inches, he would—it was possible to feel—have done so.

"And can you tell me," he said, "why the hell I should do that?"

"Oh—for the sake of a little talk, you know. Not, I need hardly say, about these unfortunate events. The sort of talk we might have had if you had managed to dine with my wife and her guests last night. Picasso, Rembrandt—things like that."

There was a moment's silence.

"Which of them chiefly?" Heffer asked.

"Oh, Rembrandt—without a doubt."

"I shall be delighted to lunch with you," Heffer said. His tone was icy. And, as he spoke, he crossed the room and picked up an umbrella and a bowler-hat.

It was against this very hat, and in this very room—Appleby remembered—that there had been perched the enigmatical painting produced by the girl who called herself Astarte Oakes.

"Astarte Oakes?" Heffer said half an hour later. The hand with which he was scooping out Stilton seemed perfectly steady. And his voice was perfectly steady too. "Yes, I remember the name."

"She brought a picture, which was examined by Gulliver and yourself?"

"Yes, she did. And we both looked at the thing. I remember the occasion very well."

"Do you, indeed?" Appleby looked hard at the young man. "One would certainly expect you too. It can scarcely be described as an incident in the remote past, you know."

"No?" For the first time, Heffer's tone was momentarily uncertain. "Perhaps it seems to me a very long time ago."

"You inspected the picture. I think you may also be said to have inspected the girl?"

Heffer raised his eyebrows slightly. The effect was to suggest that a man doesn't use expressions of that sort in speaking to a comparative stranger whom he has invited to lunch at his club.

"Inspected the girl?" Heffer said. "Is this some story which you had from Gulliver?"

"Gulliver happened to give me an account of certain events which had perplexed or struck him. He was struck, apparently, by this unknown Miss Oakes. She was strikingly beautiful or handsome?"

"Beautiful? Handsome?" Heffer looked at Appleby in urbane surprise. "Good Lord, no! She was a dim little creature, as far as I remember. No looks at all."

There was a moment's silence.

"We take coffee in another room," Appleby said. "But would you care for a glass of port with this cheese?"

"Thank you, no. But the cheese is excellent. We have nothing as good in my place." Another silence followed this polite exchange. "How very odd of Gulliver," Heffer then said. "To say that about Miss . . . Oakes, was it?"

"Oakes."

"He liked building up a bit of a romance, did poor Gulliver. I expect he made quite something out of the girl's picture, as well."

"Out of the Rembrandt? He was certainly much struck with it—as I understand you were too."

"Did you say *Rembrandt*?" Heffer sat back and laughed—a little too loudly for some of his neighbours. "And what sort of a Rembrandt did the old boy say it was? A Saskia? A Hendrickje Stoffels? A landscape? A fancy-dress scriptural affair?"

Appleby made no reply, and this time the silence prolonged itself notably.

"In point of fact," Heffer said, "what the girl brought

in was an eighteenth-century family portrait. I remember thinking for a moment that it might be by Mason
Chamberlin, who is a notable painter in an odd
eclectic way. But it wasn't. It was simply unknown
work of no particular significance or interest."

Appleby nodded absently. He was signing his bill.

"Do you know," he said, as he rose, "that unknown
work fascinates me? I just hate leaving off until I have
discovered the responsible hand. Shall we move on for
that coffee?"

But if Jimmy Heffer was hard to rattle—Appleby
reflected as he led the way to the smoking-room—it
wasn't because the young man was in any sense
unperturbed. It was rather as if he had been, so to
speak, perturbed once and for all; it was as if something had so decisively happened to him that nothing
could really ever happen to him again. And he hadn't
been like this last night. The death of Jacob Trechmann
had confronted him with some sort of crisis, put him in
some sort of dilemma. But he hadn't been then, as he
indefinably but assuredly was now, a man to whom
there had happened the kind of thing that happens for
keeps. It was the death of Gulliver, not the death of
Trechmann, that had taken Heffer across some
mysterious Rubicon.

"Would you care for a cigar?" Appleby enquired
politely, when the coffee had appeared before them.

"No, thank you." And Heffer accepted a cigarette.
"After all," he murmured ironically, "we mustn't
overdo things, must we? Even on an expense account
footed by Her Majesty's Government."

"As you please. But I don't know that you need really boggle at a cigar. Has it occurred to you that Her Majesty's Government may soon feel obliged to foot a considerably larger bill on your behalf?"

Heffer set his coffee cup down carefully.

"Meaning?" he said.

"Oh, come!" Appleby smiled and made a slight gesture with his hands. "You're not disputing, are you, that at this moment you are heading straight for a very substantial term of imprisonment?"

The mildness of this did have its effect. Heffer turned perceptibly pale. He stubbed out the cigarette, produced a cigarette-case, and lit one of his own. It was only when this symbolical action had been achieved that he spoke.

"Do you commonly," he asked, "accompany your hospitality with conversation of this kind?"

"Of course not." Appleby spoke quite simply now. "I've just been hoping, you see, that a combination of privacy and shock-tactics might induce a little wholesome frankness in your attitude to these mysterious events. I'd like to have your idea of why Trechmann was killed, and——"

"I have *no* idea of why Trechmann was killed."

"You haven't?" Appleby looked at Heffer curiously —but not at all as one who disbelieves. "That may be so. But at least you are aware of activities of Trechmann's to which he didn't—well, give much publicity."

"I am nothing of the sort."

"I confess to a slight scepticism on that point. As for Miss Oakes, either Gulliver told me what is not true yesterday, or you have told me what is not true to-day. Your accounts are irreconcilable."

"Oh, impressions vary, you know—and memory is notoriously fallible."

"That, if I may say so, is merely frivolous. You agree with Gulliver only on three material points: that the girl appeared, claimed the name of Astarte Oakes, and produced a picture. And these, as it happens, are the three points upon which irrefutable testimony exists. The girl presented herself, stated her business, and wrote her name—or wrote *a* name—in a book. The vital point, of course, is the nature of the picture. Only you and Gulliver saw it. But how many people heard of it?"

"You for a start, it seems."

"Quite so. And for a finish, too. That appears to be what you are banking on, Heffer. Isn't it rather a big risk?"

"I don't understand you."

"If I had to recount in a witness box what Gulliver told me about that picture, it might be suggested that my memory was at fault, or that my evidence was for some other reason quite inaccurate. But what if he told this story to other friends? You are simply gambling on the supposition that he did not."

"I totally fail to comprehend you."

"I don't think so. Shall I give you my sketch of the situation?"

Heffer took a watch from his waistcoat pocket and consulted it.

"As you please," he said in his most icy manner.

"Thank you. It may really save us time later. The picture was brought to you and you had a look at it.

At once you went across to Gulliver, and he went back with you to your room. Neither of you had the slightest doubt that here was a Rembrandt—a painting of quite enormous value."

"I tell you——"

"Very well, Heffer. For the moment let it be a Mason Chamberlin—or rather *not* a Mason Chamberlin, but something entirely unknown and insignificant. At least, you call in the young lady. She is shown into the presence of the Director and his assistant. I don't think she had ever seen Gulliver before, but I am quite sure that she had seen you. No, don't interrupt. You knew each other—but the girl had come in with no suspicion that here was your job and that she might run into you. So you were both a little disconcerted. Gulliver, as it happens, wasn't really aware of all this, since the picture, whatever its authorship or merits, was continuing to absorb him. But the fact, I may say, somehow seeped through his narrative."

Heffer's eyes had narrowed on Appleby. They showed cold through a haze of cigarette smoke.

"Continue," he said.

"This girl had given a false name and a false address—and for the purpose of getting an expert opinion on something that might be worth a fortune. She was naturally perturbed when she found herself identified by you. But you didn't give her away. To begin with, that may have been pure chivalry. There was this fact, of course, that she was astoundingly beautiful."

"She was as dim as a mouse."

"She was astoundingly beautiful. But now she took both her astounding beauty and her astounding picture

out of your gallery with the greatest celerity. You didn't
mind, because you knew where to find her—or at
least to hunt for her. You set about the job next day—
suddenly taking a chunk of a holiday due to you for
the purpose." Appleby paused for a moment. "Now,
let us suppose that the Rembrandt was not, in fact, the
legal property of this young person——"

"I consider that to be a derogatory and offensive
expression." Heffer had interrupted stonily. "She was
a lady, and she had better be referred to with proper
respect."

Appleby stared. It was, for some reason, a long time
since he had felt so surprised.

"This dim mouse?" he asked.

Heffer's pale face was momentarily suffused with a
flush.

"Yes," he said—stonily still—"this dim mouse."

"Very well. Suppose this girl was not the owner of
the Rembrandt, and suppose that she wanted to make
money out of it. This would be feasible only if certain
circumstances obtained. The true proprietor must be
ignorant or indifferent as to whether this canvas—
perhaps thought of as without value—were still in his
possession or not. He must never become aware of some
big deal in the picture market which he might identify
with this particular hitherto disregarded possession. Do
I make myself clear?"

"Quite as clear as most romancers contrive to be.
Go on."

"Very well. I am inclined to conjecture that an
incontestably and self-evidently genuine Rembrandt of
the first order which had *no* provenance—*no* known

previous history—could be put on the market easily enough. A story could be told about it when asked for, and nobody would bother very much. What would interest a purchaser would simply be the unhesitating endorsement of all the greatest authorities on the painter. So a Rembrandt out of the blue, so to speak, would be easy money. But suppose it couldn't be brought forward quite out of the blue and with some simple and convenient fiction attached to it. Suppose there was one man who *had* seen it before, and who *could* provide it with a scrap of authentic provenance. And suppose that that man happened to occupy a professional position such that a great Rembrandt couldn't possibly be publicly sold without his becoming aware of it, and inspecting it either in the original or in a reproduction. A Sir Gabriel Gulliver, in fact. How awkward that might be."

"Awkward?" Heffer said.

"Oh, come." Appleby paused and smiled. "I'm afraid, you know, that I'm always saying 'Oh, come.' But you do ask for it. For you can't maintain that you're not really following me."

"Very true. I'm not so much following you as preceding you, Sir John. I feel rather like some tolerably mobile creature moving through a fantastic jungle, and hearing a somewhat out-of-condition elephant crashing along behind. A policemanly elephant, but one belonging to the best clubs. Go on going on."

"Very well. I continue to crash. The question is: Ought something to be done about Gulliver? Ought Gulliver to be squared?"

Heffer gave another of the laughs that were just a shade too loud.

"The jungle becomes a bog," he said. "And the elephant goes down with a plop. For a moment there is the tip of a trunk, and then only a few bubbles before all is still. You can't imagine that anybody would seriously contemplate 'squaring', as you call it, the Director of the——"

"There might be differing views. There was something lurkingly vulnerable, something not quite stable, about Sir Gabriel Gulliver. Intelligence—or could it rather be intuition?—might bank upon that. And the brute order of money involved is a factor. One hears of £30,000, or £50,000, or $200,000 being bid for pretty well nothing at all—a canvas painted five years ago by a fellow with the output of a high-efficiency marine engine, or fifty years ago by somebody who went to tea with your grandmother."

"Very true," Heffer said. "We've found something to agree about at last."

"And an Old Master of the first quality, provided it engages the interest of the right competitors, may fetch such a sum that a mere rake-off from the total would rate as a substantial private fortune."

This time Heffer was silent.

"So we mustn't laugh out of court the notion of squaring Gabriel Gulliver. One might indulge it. One might feel one had glimpsed some weakness in the man. One might go forward on that basis. And one might find, too late, that one had been all wrong."

"Too late?" Heffer said. He was now as pale as a sheet.

"Just that. One might have burned one's boats."

"And then?"

"Well—something rather definitive might happen."

"And *then*?" Heffer had stood up, like a man who is about to take his leave.

Appleby got up too, and led his guest from the room.

"To that one," he said, "the answer can only come from you."

"One would have to fight," Heffer said. He spoke with a quiet, cold finality, which was yet oddly touching. "There would be nothing for it but that."

CHAPTER ELEVEN

FAIR WARNING—APPLEBY thought, as he turned away from the door to which he had conducted his guest. I gave him fair warning. Did he give it to me too?

There is a good deal that I don't believe about Jimmy Heffer—he told himself, making his way back through the club. The question is: Does my disbelief extend one point too far? I'd know a good deal more— probably a great deal more—if I could just contact the girl who called herself Astarte Oakes. And there can't be all that many absolute Botticelli Venuses in England. Perhaps I'll know her when I see her.

He turned into the little reading-room. *Silence is observed*. A voice, however, spoke to him at once.

"Hullo, Appleby. That was a most delightful dinner-party last night."

"We were so pleased that you were able to come." As he made this conventional reply, Appleby saw that Carl Bendixson had lowered a newspaper and appeared to propose conversation.

"Shocking news about Gabriel Gulliver," Bendixson said. "Only just heard it. Fellow told me as I came across the hall."

"Yes," Appleby said. "Shocking."

"Shot in his own fastness! It seems incredible. And not thought to be a matter of robbery, I'm told. Have they caught the chap who did it?"

"Chap?" Appleby said.

"A madman, or I wouldn't be surprised. I shall positively tremble the next time I get up on my little rostrum and bang my little hammer." Bendixson laughed—not entirely easily. "Make a damned good target."

"There will be a clear motive in your case." Appleby appeared willing to talk nonsense. "A disgruntled bidder, who feels you failed to catch his nod—or that you caught it once too often."

"Yes, yes." Bendixson assumed the whimsical expression of one who indulges in meaningless self-depreciation. "I live by coaxing out of people more money than they mean to give. Nothing could be more impossibly debased. I knocked down a very indifferent Romney portrait this morning for you wouldn't believe how much. And—do you know?—I positively caught the fellow on the canvas curling his aristocratic lip at me. I wish I auctioned fat cattle or the residual effects of bankrupt greengrocers."

"No," Appleby said. "You don't. It wouldn't be so lucrative. And it wouldn't be such fun."

"Too true." And Bendixson sighed resignedly. "But talking of fun, isn't Mary Wildsmith delightful? Gretta and I always adore the opportunity of meeting her."

"Yes, quite delightful." Appleby decided that he would give not more than a further two minutes to this twaddle. "But I don't often see her on the stage," he said—this merely because a sentence or two of further small-talk must be found. "Judith said something about her being a good deal in France. I gathered that she is

French on her mother's side. No doubt that's part of
the charm."

"No doubt. And, now you mention it, I believe she
goes over occasionally to do character parts on their
radio or television or something. Little Anglo-French
comedies."

"Ah, yes. I wonder whether she was by any chance a
friend of Gulliver's?" Appleby couldn't have told why
he asked this question. Perhaps it was just long habit
in trying to link up one thing with another.

"Not that I know of." Bendixson gave what might
have been called a well-informed laugh. "He had his
favourites, or so one has been told. But I doubt whether
Mary was one of them. But a chap she does know there
is young Jimmy Heffer. Do you know him?"

"I'm beginning to." Civility satisfied, Appleby was
moving towards the door. Then he remembered something. "By the way," he said, "there's something with
which you might help me. Would you describe yourself
as good at eyes?"

Bendixson stared.

"At making them, you mean? What Shakespeare
calls strange œiliads and most speaking looks?"

"No—at recognizing them." Appleby had produced
his pocket-book, and from this he drew the scrap of
paper which he had rescued from a Bloomsbury garbage bin. He handed it to Bendixson. "Can you place
that?"

"Is this a new parlour game?" Bendixson was looking idly at the fragmentary eye. "Something to replace
jig-saw puzzles?"

Appleby laughed.

"It's detective investigation, as a matter of fact. Somebody tore up a colour-print, and this scrap happens to survive. The problem is to identify the print."

Bendixson looked mildly embarrassed. And this was clearly because the problem was so simple that nobody of moderate general cultivation ought to be held up by it.

"Only Van Gogh," he said, "ever painted an eye in that way." And he handed the scrap back to Appleby.

"Well, that's fine. And the queer thing is that—even while I didn't see what you've now told me—I felt familiar with the thing. Can you name the actual painting? Oddly enough, it was a question I was minded to put to Gulliver."

Bendixson nodded absently. He thought for a moment.

"I'm no authority on Van Gogh—Lord knows," he said. "I don't even like the man. But—yes—I can see the picture. It's a self-portrait, painted round about 1886. And now it's knocking about the Mediterranean, on board some millionaire's damned brassy yacht."

"I don't think I've ever been on board a millionaire's damned brassy yacht. And yet I have this feeling that it's familiar to me. So that would be in a reproduction too."

"No doubt. It's a familiar print, I think." Bendixson hesitated. "Is it permissible to ask how such a thing can be of any interest to you professionally?"

"A lot of odd things are." For a moment Appleby let this reply serve. "I'd like to know who owned the print, and where it ultimately came from."

"It doesn't sound easy. But let me look at it again." Bendixson took the scrap and examined it more carefully this time. "You want the opinion of a first-class print-seller," he said. "But I think I know what he'll tell you. It's an absolutely tip-top job. German, probably. The Germans do most of the best things that have high-grade optical work behind them. Almost depressing—the excellence of this sort of stuff nowadays. Science catching up on inspiration, and so forth." Bendixson offered this lazy bit of thinking with a suitable air of laziness. And he picked up his newspaper again. "*Do* tell your wife how much we enjoyed it," he said.

"She'll be delighted," Appleby said. And he went out of the room.

It was only to collide, however, with somebody in the doorway. And the newcomer, having glanced past him, drew back.

"That that fellow Bendixson?" the newcomer murmured.

Appleby shut the door.

"Yes," he said. "Bendixson. He's in process of recovering from a disdainful look cast at him by a Romney."

"I'm dashed if I want to see the beggar. Only the other day he made me pay the deuce of a lot for a Toulouse-Lautrec."

Appleby laughed.

"My dear fellow—if you must please yourself with buying these fashionable things, what are you to expect? Not even shipping will stand it for long."

The newcomer—his name was Moultrie and he was a very wealthy man indeed—nodded gloomily.

"True," he said. "Absolutely true. It's a mug's game. I wish I'd taken up postage stamps."

"You don't wish anything of the sort." The two men were now strolling down a corridor, "I can see that you're just stuffing with satisfaction over your blessed Toulouse-Lautrec. Of course that's nothing singular in this club. A place more reeking of acquisitive instinct doesn't exist in London. How I drifted into it, I just can't think."

"Beer-mugs dug up at Stonehenge, I've been told. Haven't you more of them than any other man in the country? So I've been assured." Moultrie was evidently in high good humour. "And as for this new picture of mine, I'm not at all sure. There seem to be rather a lot of the little devil's canvases about."

"Ah," Appleby said. "Doubt about the scarcity value. Well, well."

"You think of me, Appleby, just as another damned commercial man." Moultrie was genially unoffended. "But in fact I have a passion for the artistic life. I don't merely buy these things. I read about the chaps who made them. It's a world full of horror and romance and all the rest of it. This fellow Lautrec, for instance, that Bendixson has peddled me——"

"Peddled you?" Appleby was interested. "You mean he sold you this painting privately? You didn't get it at auction through his firm?"

"Just that. And I've paid, as I said, a damned sight too much. But that was because of the romantic slant on the affair—which is what I was getting round to

telling you. Not that I *ought* to tell you. Bendixson
wouldn't approve."

"Silence is observed," Appleby said.

"What's that? Oh, I see." Moultrie had sat down
on a somewhat decayed leather settee in the corridor,
and he gestured to Appleby to do the same. "But,
since I've started, here goes. Lautrec, you remember,
was a shocking little slobbering dwarf. Tough on him.
Old aristocratic French family, you know, with men
who thought mostly about hunting and hawking and
capturing women. But for this wretched little cripple
all that was out. So he became a painter. Amazing
thing."

"Amazing thing," Appleby said.

"Tremendous virility, the little chap had. Awkward
for him. But it seems that talented women gave him a
spin now and then. Suzanne Valadon, for example.
I've got her. Of course she wasn't anything like the
painter her illegitimate son was. Utrillo, you know.
I've got him too. Middle period, before his brain and
his painting went soft."

"That's splendid," Appleby said.

"Lautrec's life was mostly brothels and drink. A
terrible story, really terrible. Died at thirty-seven.
D.T's, and the inevitable sort of disease. Quite shocking. During his last year or two his work went off badly
—except for one notable period of recovery. But perhaps
you know all this."

"I don't know about the notable period of recovery,"
Appleby said. He was finding the tone of this talk rather
hideous. But instinct prevented him from breaking it
off.

"Exactly!" Moultrie's voice had a ring of triumph which was only too familiar to Appleby. It went with collector's mania. "It happened here in London, as a matter of fact. Lautrec came here from time to time. His English was good, and he liked it. Sometimes he went round with friends among the English painters. They would take him to see Oscar Wilde, and that sort of thing. But sometimes he'd come and just wander around in solitude, like a lost soul. His last visit—it seems to have escaped his biographers—was like that. But then, one day in the British Museum, he met this girl."

"This girl?" Appleby repeated. He had a sudden fascinated sense of the direction in which Moultrie was taking him.

"A French girl, as a matter of fact. Her name was Armandine de la Gallette——"

"It was *what*?"

"Armandine de la Gallette. A noble but impoverished family, it seems, and the girl had taken a job as a governess in the household of some English lord or duke. But she had seen Lautrec's work in Paris, and she revered his genius."

"So she set about saving him?"

"Just that." Moultrie appeared impressed by this perceptive question. "She was what poor Lautrec had always dreamed of: a pure and cultivated woman who was not revolted by his physical appearance. They spent three weeks at Rye together, before Armandine's people heard of the affair and insisted on bringing her home. She was only nineteen."

"I see. And in those three weeks Lautrec painted your picture."

"Exactly, Appleby." Moultrie was again struck by this penetration. "It's called *Femme assise*. 'Seated Woman', you know. Needless to say, it's of Armandine de la Gallette herself. And I don't think it's too much to say that it's Lautrec's masterpiece." Moultrie paused. "I certainly hope it is," he added, a little wistfully. "For there's no doubt I paid the devil of a price. I only wish that poor Armandine had got the money. She's quite, quite charming."

Appleby stared.

"You mean she's *alive*? Didn't Toulouse-Lautrec die in about 1900?"

"1901. Armandine must be nearly eighty. The fascinating thing is that she's quite recognizable in the portrait. It gave me a turn, that did, I'm bound to say."

"It certainly gives a touch of refinement to the whole affair. You say the painting wasn't in her possession?"

"No. It was in the hands of a private collector, who didn't want to be known. That was why Carl Bendixson fixed it up that I should actually see the old lady and question her. It fixed the provenance of the painting so securely."

" 'Fixed' seems just the word." Appleby was staring at Moultrie rather grimly. "Where did you see her?"

"A little place in the New Forest, Winterbourne Crucis. She has a cottage. Rose Cottage, it's called. Rather commonplace, eh? But the interior's a dream."

"A dream? Well, well." Appleby was now looking rather wonderingly at this captain of industry. "How has Armandine come to end up there? I thought her people had taken her home."

"So they had. But she was always very Anglophile. When she came into a minute private fortune, she decided to retire into the English countryside. She brought a few sticks of furniture with her. The finest eighteenth century French stuff. But the rest of the place is quite bare. It's too touching. And—do you know?—I rather took advantage of her being so poor. Not that I didn't give her a terrific price."

"I thought you said——"

"Oh, not for the painting. All she could do was to tell me the story of that. What she sold me was her last relic of Lautrec. His famous walking-stick flask."

Appleby found himself taking a deep breath.

"You astonish me," he said.

"You see, when Lautrec was a hopeless alcoholic, his family provided him with a keeper. Some sort of poor relation who went round with him and had the job of keeping him off the bottle. So Lautrec had this walking-stick made. Hollow, you know, and would hold half a litre of brandy. At Rye, the poor chap believed that Armandine had reformed him for good. So he presented her with the thing. Too sad, eh? And I could see that the whole business of bringing up the past was extremely painful to the old lady. In fact, she made me promise something. You'd never guess what."

"Not to visit her again."

"You're absolutely right. Remarkable knowledge of human nature you have, my dear chap." Moultrie was looking at Appleby with deep respect. "And, of course,

I'll keep my word to her. I shall find the whole episode rather a beautiful memory."

"And so will she, I don't doubt." Appleby stood up. "By the way, have you ever been to Albi?"

"Albi? Where's that?"

"About fifty miles from Toulouse. I seem to remember that it has some associations with Lautrec."

"Oh, a place in France. No—you know, I hardly ever go abroad. I simply haven't the time, my dear fellow." Suddenly Moultrie gave Appleby his rather wistful and uncertain smile. "Well, what do you think of my yarn?"

"What do I think?" Appleby, in return, was quite unsmiling. "I think that those whom the gods wish to destroy, they first make mad. Just a little mad, for a start. Inclined, say, to unseasonable jokes in the course of business. But later—well, very mad indeed."

CHAPTER TWELVE

IT WAS BARELY half-past two, and there were still plenty of lunchers lingering in the club. This gave Appleby an idea. Before putting it into execution, however, he went to the telephone-room, shut himself firmly in, and called Judith.

"Busy?" he asked.

"Not in *your* sense, darling. Of course the little woman has her small employments about the house. Dusting hubby's study—or is it den?—without disturbing the litter. Beginning to think about something tasty for his——"

"Stop it. I'm in a hurry. Do you think you could get to a place in the New Forest and back by dinner-time?"

"I might. What place?"

"It's called Winterbourne Crucis. I seem to remember it vaguely. You find out about Rose Cottage. Whether it's inhabited, and by whom. If it's not, whether it's furnished or empty. Previous tenants. Village worthies who worked there. Everything."

"It sounds as if it were a horrid little love-nest."

"Don't be absurd. I keep a special sort of copper for investigating that. This looks like being something rather curious."

"All right, John. Can do." Judith was mollified. "But hadn't I better be put in the picture?"

"The picture? Well, there certainly is a picture. By Toulouse-Lautrec."

"John, what on earth are you talking about?"

"Toulouse-Lautrec. I've just met a man who recently bought one—or believes he did. And he authenticated it by going to this Rose Cottage, Winterbourne Crucis, and interviewing Lautrec's sitter. Does that sound like nonsense?"

"I don't know." Judith was properly cautious. "Is he supposed to have painted this person down there?"

"No. Probably in London. It was of a girl who befriended him in his last years, and who came to England again later. It couldn't, I think, be later than 1897 or 1898."

"I've got a book about Lautrec. What was the girl's name?"

"Armandine de la Gallette. What do you think of that?"

Judith's laughter crackled in the receiver.

"It must be some sort of hoax, John. The Moulin de la Gallette was one of the early cabarets in Montmartre. That would be Lautrec's real tie-up with the name."

"Quite so. It rang that sort of bell in my head at once. And the chap believes himself to have obtained a relic of Lautrec actually in the museum at Albi! But this business is more than a hoax, I think. It looks like large-scale fraud—and perhaps something else as well. So discover what you can."

"All right. But hadn't I better know who is supposed to be perpetrating this fraud?"

"I've nothing but a wild suspicion at the moment, I'm afraid. But it has just occurred to me——" Appleby broke off, realizing that somebody was about to enter the telephone-room. "No good," he said. "We'll have it all out at dinner-time." And he rang off.

Five minutes later, Judith Appleby was making a telephone-call of her own.

"I hate to be a nuisance," she said. "But do you remember borrowing a book about Toulouse-Lautrec a couple of months ago?"

"But of course I do!" The voice at the other end was enthusiastic. "It was intensely interesting. And have I hung on to it? But how unforgivable of me. I am most terribly sorry. Let me bring it round at once."

"Certainly not!" Judith was emphatic. "I feel bad about bothering you. It's just that I have occasion to look something up in it. Listen. I'm running down to the New Forest, to a place called Winterbourne Crucis. I'll be passing your way in ten minutes. Do you mind if I stop and pick it up?"

"But of course. I'll have it ready for you."

"Thank you so much. That's fine."

"Indeed it *is*," the voice said. "And *so* nice of you to ring up first."

Appleby had gone upstairs to the great drawing-room. It was the place in which his more genuinely leisured fellow-members tended to forgather. Time itself seemed to take on a richer amplitude in this august chamber.

But Appleby himself had a good deal of work on hand. He couldn't afford to draw too many blanks. Well, there in a corner by himself, lost in reflection and

seeming far from approachable, was Lord Mountmerton. He was the biggest of the lot. If he left his
pictures to the Tate—and he was an old man now—
the Tate would have to let itself out at the seams.
Appleby walked across the room and sat down beside
Lord Mountmerton. Lord Mountmerton greeted him
with extreme courtesy. It was the old boy's way of
showing as much surprise as it was admissible for one
member to show on being thus accosted by another,
much his junior.

"Henry James," Appleby said, easily and vaguely.
"I've just discovered that we have a constable in the
police force called Henry James. It struck me as
odd."

"Two perfectly common English names." Lord
Mountmerton, not altogether unnaturally, was unim-
pressed. "The odd thing is that he should be an
Irishman."

"My constable?"

"No, no—the novelist. As so many Americans
are. His people, you know, came from County
Cavan."

"I didn't know that." Appleby managed to sound
like one who has been usefully instructed. "Did you
ever meet him?"

"I think not. He went out a great deal, one reads.
But not among the right people. That is apparent from
his books. He moved among snobs."

"Didn't he move among artists?"

"Very indifferently. Very indifferently, indeed. You
no doubt know that strangest of his productions, *The
Golden Bowl*. An American of enormous wealth is

represented as devoted to art. He forms a great collection, proposing to present it to some obscure provincial city in the United States. But his passion never takes him within hail of a living artist. He simply frequents dealers, and buys the work of painters long dead. That is not, to my mind, to fulfil the duties of a patron of the arts."

"Your own personal acquaintance with artists must stretch pretty far back?"

"I knew Monet, Degas and Renoir."

"And Manet?"

"I am not Methuselah, my dear sir. Manet died in 1883."

Appleby was suitably abashed.

"However," Lord Mountmerton continued courteously, "my father once had some conversation with Manet. Manet was something of a dandy, it seems, but civil enough."

Appleby laughed.

"I can imagine," he said, "Cosimo de' Medici saying something like that about Michelozzo. And adding that the fellow had built him a very decent library."

Lord Mountmerton sat up. He seemed for the first time to be really emerging from abstraction.

"Why," he asked, "do you come across and rally me like this—an old man as I am, with matters to reflect on which are important to myself?"

This was intimidating. But now Appleby had to go ahead.

"Because," he said, "I am, like the youngest Henry James, a policeman——"

"Yes, yes—I am aware of that. You appear to control, if I may say so, a very respectable body of men."

"Thank you. And I am minded to make an appeal to you. Perhaps you have heard of the death of Sir Gabriel Gulliver?"

"Dear me, no."

"He was shot dead in his office this morning."

"I am sorry to hear it. He was a very considerable authority in his field. A scholar, in fact." Lord Mountmerton made this acknowledgement with gravity. "But my acquaintance with him was slight. It is scarcely to be conceived that I can be of assistance to you."

"I think it possible that you can. Gulliver's death appears to have taken place on the fringes of some very considerable fraudulent operation in the field of connoisseurship and art-collecting."

"Fraud?" Lord Mountmerton raised his eyebrows. "You can hardly suppose anything of that sort to come my way."

"Of course not. What I really want is the benefit of your experience in the business of authenticating works of art created—or supposed to have been created—round about the turn of the century. When it is a question of Old Masters, I know, it is nowadays largely a matter for scientists——"

"That is mostly nonsense, my dear sir." It was clear from Lord Mountmerton's tone that Appleby had decidely put a foot wrong here. "In such matters there is no substitute for sound connoisseurship—no substitute whatever. Competent expertise is still based on the work of Morelli in the seventies, not on infra-red photography and all the rest of it. The elements remain what they were. How did Bramantino model the lobe of an ear? How did Lorenzo Costa paint a cuticle? It is upon the fine discrimination of such minutiae that the whole fabric of our knowledge rests."

"I see," Appleby said. He was rather wishing that he had gone straight back to Scotland Yard. There might be news by now of where Jimmy Heffer had headed for after his uncomfortable lunch. Appleby was putting a good deal of hope in that.

"But of course with the modern masters," Lord Mountmerton was saying, "our problem is less one of attribution than of authentication. I am in agreement with you there. It is all a matter of provenance."

"Just so," Appleby said. His interest was quickening again. "I imagine you have often bought pictures direct from the studios of Renoir and the rest of them?"

"Dear me, yes."

"And from the heirs and executors, and so forth, of similar painters not long dead?"

"Certainly, certainly."

"You would feel fairly secure in dealing with a widow, or a son. But there must have been marginal cases? I mean, you at times have been offered paintings vouched for as genuine by persons rather uncertainly related to the artist?"

"Possibly so, possibly so." Lord Mountmerton's expression, if observed upon features less august, would have been described as going cagey. "Yes—possibly so."

"I assure you," Appleby said, "that this is a serious

enquiry, made in the interest of justice. Has there been
any occasion within recent years in which you have
made a purchase in this way—that is, through some
personal connection of the painter's, and more or less
confidentially—upon which you have later come to
look back with any misgiving?"

"Meaning," Lord Mountmerton said, "with some
suspicion that I had been duped? It wouldn't be easy,
you know. I am old. I do not suppose myself to be a
man of very high intelligence, such as my father was.
But I have a great deal of experience. It would not be
easy to dupe me in an art deal."

"That might make it all the more exciting to try.
The fascination of what's difficult, as some poet says."

Lord Mountmerton frowned.

"Do criminals," he asked, "court risks in a sporting
spirit?"

"Indeed they do. Their temperament is often close
to that of the gambler—particularly in what may be
called the higher reaches of crime. It would be fun to
sell a fake to Lord Mountmerton."

"I suppose it would." Lord Mountmerton said this
with something less than his accustomed austerity. He
had been tickled by this vision of himself as a sort of
Mount Everest among victims of criminal guile. "But
I cannot be confident," he added, "that it has ever
happened to me."

"Can you be confident that it has *not*?"

"That is a different question."

"Do you, at this moment, possess any picture,
acquired in the manner we have been considering,
about which you now feel any doubts?"

Tackled point-blank in this way, Lord Mountmerton was silent for a moment. Once more, Appleby was faced with the instinct to clam up which is so tiresome an element in the collector's psychology. But then Lord Mountmerton spoke.

"I have to confess," he said, "to a certain element of doubt about my last Van Gogh."

Appleby took a quick glance around him. There were still a few men lingering in what the club called its drawing-room. But the vastness of the place was such that this conversation couldn't possibly be overheard.

"You heard of this Van Gogh," he asked cautiously, "through some private source connected with the painter himself?"

"I bought it from such a source. Vincent Van Gogh, as you must know, fought a losing battle against insanity, and made away with himself in 1900, at the age of thirty-seven. He had only once or twice succeeded in selling a picture—and this in spite of the fact that his brother, Théo Van Gogh, was manager of a gallery in the Boulevard Montmartre. A few months after Vincent's death, Théo went mad in his turn. He was taken back to Holland, and died a few weeks later in an asylum at Utrecht. On the Continent, as in England, it had been a tragic generation for the arts. That, however, is not our present concern. The morals of all these people were not as yours or mine. It seems that, as a very young man, Théo Van Gogh had formed a liaison with an improper female."

"Ah," Appleby said.

"There was a son of this irregular union. He remained in France, took the respectable name of Bontemps, and became a moderately prosperous notary in Autun. He inherited from his father—by will, as it had to be—a number of his uncle's miscellaneous effects. These passed to his only daughter, who had married a grocer, bookseller and stationer called Borange, also of Autun. There was nothing of much importance—with one single exception. That exception was a large canvas, painted at Arles."

"And you bought it from this Mme Borange?"

"Precisely."

"In circumstances of some confidence?"

"Certainly." Lord Mountmerton paused. "I need not, perhaps, assure you that there was no question of buying quietly an article the full value of which was not known to the owner. Mme Borange knew what she possessed, and she was as shrewd at driving a bargain as was her husband, the *petit épicier*. But she wanted no 'publicity', as the current phrase has it. Artistic connections, it seems, are not regarded as advantageous in the *ambiance* of the Boranges of Autun. A connection in the *Institut*, indeed, might be one thing. But two mad brothers—Dutchmen at that—only a couple of generations back was quite another. Mme Borange made her conditions."

"You were not to seek her out again, and you were not to send others to do so?"

Lord Mountmerton was silent for a moment.

"The tenor of our conversation has been such," he said presently, "that I cannot affect to be surprised by your final question."

"In fact, Lord Mountmerton, you were had?"

"Had?" Lord Mountmerton appeared to consider this brutal colloquialism fairly. "I am dissatisfied with the picture. I have not hung it."

"But you haven't thought to go back to Autun and investigate?"

"Certainly not. I gave this grocer's wife my word."

"I see." Appleby was staring hard at Lord Mountmerton. If you are one of the wealthiest men in England, he thought, it's open to you to carry a point of honour to the farthest extreme. Or was it conceivable that, rather than expose himself as having been successfully duped, Lord Mountmerton had been prepared to cut his losses and forget the matter? Thirty thousand pounds had become a sort of standard figure for deals of this sort—the deals that you might rate as of secondary or tertiary importance. It would be something of that order that the lady calling herself Mme Borange had got away with. You could mount quite a show in return for that much, and still have a very pretty profit at the end of it.

"It's most kind of you to tell me this," Appleby said. "And I shall, of course, regard it as entirely confidential. But, as you may guess, there is one other question I want to ask you. How did you hear of Mme Borange in the first place?"

This time it was Lord Mountmerton who looked round the room.

"There," he said, "we come to another difficulty I should have faced in pursuing my misgivings. The person who gave me, as they say, a 'line' on Mme

Borange was of the most unchallengeable standing in the art world."

"Was it——" Appleby checked himself. It wasn't his habit to prompt people.

"It was somebody I shall never question now. My informant was Gabriel Gulliver."

CHAPTER THIRTEEN

As Appleby came down the steps of the club he saw that his own car was standing at the kerb. There could be only one explanation of that. He stepped into it, flicked a switch, and was instantly listening to the impassive voice of Parker.

"You there, sir? I thought I'd better get you this way. It's moving."

"Is it, indeed?" Appleby spoke to the air at large. "Then I'll get moving too."

"Cornhill for a start, sir."

Appleby leant forward and spoke to his chauffeur.

"Cornhill," he said. "But don't kill anybody. We're not on the telly yet."

"No, sir." The man was inured to the Commissioner's primitive sense of humour. The car glided off in the direction of Trafalgar Square. Appleby closed a window, and the noise of traffic faded to a murmur.

"Well?" he said.

"It looks as if it paid off, sir." Parker's voice was judiciously admiring. "Letting Heffer have his head, I mean. Of course we had a man waiting to trail him when he left your club. Straight from the telly, *he* was. You'd have placed him a mile away."

Appleby laughed.

"Child's play, Parker. And then?"

"Heffer walked up to Piccadilly Circus and put in some nice work in the subway. Our man was baffled.

Heffer's last glimpse of him must have been very comforting. Standing by the Gents and looking anxiously in the wrong direction . . . Leadenhall Street."

"Leadenhall Street," Appleby said to the chauffeur. "And then?"

"Heffer made for the bombed site just off Cambridge Circus. That's where he keeps his car during the day. I'd discovered that already—so Heffer had a little trouble in getting out. Somebody else had parked far too close to him."

"Excellent," Appleby said. It would have been uncharitable to seem unacceptive of these unnecessary details. "Your second man had no difficulty in following him there?"

"None at all. And I made it just as Heffer drove out. I'm in the greengrocer's van . . . Aldgate High Street."

"Aldgate High Street? It sounds as if he's going out the Mile End Road."

"Yes, sir. Hullo! He's stopped. Telephone kiosk. Going to make a call. Tricky bit for us. No—we've pulled in behind a stationary lorry."

"Can you spare somebody to get out and trace the call, Parker?"

"Yes, sir. Three of us here. Telephone Exchange will get the answer to the Yard, and the Yard will get it back to me in the van. All before Heffer's made another couple of miles—if he's going as far as that."

"We'll hope that Heffer is telephoning ahead, to make sure of the girl he's going after."

"Girl, sir?"

"Yes, Parker. I'll be upset if it isn't a girl—an astoundingly beautiful girl."

"Indeed, sir." Parker clearly wasn't sure that this wasn't frivolity. "Now he's out again. Quick work. Nothing in the nature of a long lovers' chat—girl or no girl. And he's going along A.11, all right. Switching to the Yard now, sir. Call you back in ten minutes. You'll be lucky if you've made this point by then. Turn you grey, this traffic would."

Appleby sat back and waited. The car nosed its way down Fleet Street. Occasionally an alert constable spotted it and managed a great air of speeding it on its journey. But it was slow work. They certainly weren't going to kill anybody. Judith, it was to be hoped, was making better speed to Winterbourne Crucis. She was a fast driver but a skilful one. She wouldn't run into any trouble. She never did.

The chauffeur, brought to a standstill in a traffic block, spoke over his shoulder.

"Like old times, this must be for you, sir."

"Well, yes—it is." Appleby was pleased. He liked to think that, in however small a way, he had his legend.

"Parker here."

"Yes?"

"We're booked for beyond Woodford, sir. Right in the Forest, in fact. If it can be called that."

"Dear me. What a bosky afternoon. My wife's on her way to a forest too. The New Forest. Which, incidentally, is older than Epping."

"Yes, sir." Parker was patient. "I've turned up Whipps Cross Road. No point in trailing him now. He might become aware that this van has been on his horizon for some time."

"Quite right. What more?"

"Well, sir, the name is Kipper."

"Parker, I don't believe it. Astarte simply can't be Miss Kipper. It would be intolerable."

"I don't know anything about that, sir." Parker's voice was now openly reproachful.

"I'm sorry, Parker. All this has been happening rather too rapidly for much talk. But I've got quite a tale for you. You did say Kipper?"

"Yes, sir. A Mrs Kipper, Veere House, Sewardstone-bury."

"*What!*" Now Appleby gave what was virtually a shout. "Spell that."

"Spell it, sir? S-E-W——"

"No, no, man. The name of the house."

"V-E-E-R-E. I made them spell it out myself. But it isn't my idea of spelling Vere."

"Ah—you're thinking of Lady Clara Vere de Vere, Parker. I'm thinking of Miss Kipper. Blessed name! I see it now. And we're right in the target area. *Avanti!*"

"Very good, sir."

Appleby, although suddenly in high spirits, was abashed. When Parker used that aggressively subordinate expression it meant that he was definitely offended.

"Listen," Appleby said. "Veere is a place on the Dutch island of Walchern. It has very ancient trading associations with both England and Scotland. And Kipper can only be a name of Dutch origin. A couple of hundred years ago it was probably Kuyper."

"Well, sir?"

"And this chase, you see, is all a matter of a Dutch picture."

"I'd never have suspected it, sir." The disembodied voice of Parker was once more merely resigned.

"A Rembrandt, as a matter of fact. And, within the next hour, I'm going to set eyes on it, or——" Appleby paused. "Well—or I'm a Dutchman!"

But perhaps I am—Appleby thought, as his car ran down the Mile End Road. If I took the next turn to the right I'd be in Stepney—where that wretched lad used his boots. I've kept an eye on that from my desk, but it hasn't occured to me to go barging in. Yet I am barging in on the Trechmann and Gulliver affair. Of course, I can plead that it has rather barged in on me. Yes—that's the point I must stress to this excellent Parker.

The car braked smoothly as an ambulance passed ahead of it with a clanging bell. The London Hospital. . . . It's nearly all tolerably clear—he told himself, sitting back. There are two stories, and I can now pin-point the place at which they intersect. What chiefly remains baffling is a purely psychological matter. It comes to this—that the Gribble affair is disconcertingly out of scale.

Moultrie had been sold a Toulouse-Lautrec and Lord Mountmerton had been sold a Van Gogh. The technique had been almost identical in each case. And it was an uncommonly good technique. Given that the faker could do his stuff and the supposed female relict of the painter in question could do her stuff, the thing

was almost foolproof. At least it was almost foolproof
if the dupes were chosen with a little circumspection.
And there were plenty of dupes. Two continents were
prolific in them. Probably there had been successful
dealings, too, in spurious Cézannes, Renoirs, Pissarros.
Sisleys and what-have-you.

Queen Mary College—a sombre haunt of the Muses
—went past on his left. Parker and his greengrocer's
van would probably have reached Veere House by
now. Parker wouldn't do more than keep it under observation. It was Appleby's rôle, clearly, to drive up
and effect a comfortable elucidation of the whole affair.

Gribble, then. Victims like Moultrie and Mountmerton would yield a fortune in no time—and there
could be rational calculation in the view that one might
get away with half a dozen or a dozen such *coups*
without disaster. But the defrauding of Gribble had
represented no less a risk than any of the other opera-
tions. And it had been undertaken for mere chicken-
feed. In fact, for £800. And the forgery, moreover, was
in a totally different medium—that of literary manuscript. Whatever the ingenuity brought to bear in this
field, the proceeds could never come to a tithe of those
gained from the faking of paintings. Again, consider
what had been forged. Gribble had believed himself to
be buying a forgery, and so he had been—in a ludi-
crous double measure. In fact there was a freakish sense
of humour behind the Manallace fraud, and it had been
indulging itself at only a negligible prompting in point
of financial gain. Conceit and whimsy, you might say,
had enjoyed a field-day at the expense of poor old
Charles Gribble. Yet the joke had ended in murder.

The obvious conclusion appeared to be that Jacob Trechmann had acted as agent for two independent crooks, or gangs of crooks. Yet even this didn't quite make sense. If he was in on the picture-racket—no doubt as one who could make valuable contacts with potential clients—why should he willingly traffic as well in very small beer, with all the increased risks attending it?

But there was another material point. Armandine de la Gallette. Moultrie was a stay-at-home chap. He would never have heard of the Moulin de la Gallette— and much less of the slang sense of this term which might suggest that poor Lautrec's supposed good angel had been a gold-digger. Nevertheless the pitching in of this wanton absurdity had been not without some hazard. Here, in fact, in a context of large stakes and large skill, was the same sort of conceited freakishness that had forged—or caused the forging of—a Manallace forgery. And it would require a strong will, surely, to foist this element of gratuitous risk upon associates in a big-time criminal organization. So here—one might say at a guess—was the master-mind.

But indeed—Appleby asked himself, as his car swung into Woodford New Road—was "freakish" quite the word that was required?

Might it not rather be "mad"?

CHAPTER FOURTEEN

"A MADWOMAN, IT seems," Parker said.

"No, no, Parker. Not a flagrant red-herring like that, please." Appleby checked himself. "Very good show," he said, with an approving nod.

"Thank you, sir. Sergeant Murray here did a thoroughly sound job at the wheel. And it's he who has found out a little about the place. He walked back to a pub on the edge of the common. It seems they know the owner of Veere House as the mad Mrs Kipper. Or, rather, they don't know her. Because nobody ever sets eyes on her. Or hears about her."

"No servants to gossip?"

"The last are said to have cleared out a couple of years ago. And I'm not surprised. Never saw a more dismal-looking place. Just take a glance up the drive, sir."

Appleby did as he was told—making his observation cautiously from behind a decayed stone pillar on which there must once have hung a gate.

"Superior old house once," he said. "Older than most of what's around here."

"It was there when its only neighbours were high-waymen, I shouldn't be surprised. What they call Queen Anne, isn't it?"

Appleby nodded.

"I suppose so. Interesting that you should get an old-established Dutch mercantile family here. Matter of the route to Harwich, I suppose."

"You seem very sure about this, sir."

"Ah—I'm doing no more than bolstering my confidence, perhaps." Appleby made another reconnaisance round the pillar. "Dismal enough, I must say."

"God-forsaken part of the world anyway, if you ask me. Neither one thing nor another. A land of litter and unenterprising picnics, I'd call it."

"A thoroughly apt description." Appleby was impressed by this flight on Parker's part. "But my guess is that this house is on the site of an old hunting-lodge. You're sure our young man is inside?"

"Well, sir, you can just see the tail-end of his car. But I've been wondering whether I should call out some of the local men and get the place surrounded. After all, it's homicide we're dealing with."

"Very true. But I don't think we'll do that yet, all the same. Only you might send your driver—Murray, did you say?—round to keep an eye on the back. And you yourself stay here by the van."

"As you please, sir." It was evident that Parker didn't approve.

"I don't want to create alarm, so you'll forgive me if I just walk up to the house by myself. Nobody come or gone since you arrived?"

"Well, yes. A fellow drove up about ten minutes ago. I think he's parked his car just in front of Heffer's. Seemed to be in rather a hurry. Looked as if he might have been a doctor."

"Did he, indeed? Well, wait for me, Parker—there's a good chap." And Appleby walked round the mouldering pillar and up the drive. He stopped, however, at a word from Parker behind him.

"One thing I forgot, sir. About what they told Murray at the pub. The only other inhabitant's a girl. A niece, she's thought to be."

"Miss Kipper, in fact?"

"That may well be, sir."

"Splendid. This affair is going to offer one sheerly aesthetic moment, at least. I look forward to it."

And Appleby walked on.

The drive was completely untended. It passed between ragged shrubberies and skirted a garden which was a wilderness. But even this hardly prepared one for the spectacle that the house itself presented on a closer view. It stood, as it were, knee-deep in weeds—like some forlorn prehistoric creature in an inedible pasture. Its grey surfaces were flaked and cracked; its woodwork was denuded of paint; many of the lower windows showed tattered curtains pulled awry, and some of the upper ones lacked entire panes of glass. The effect was the more shocking because the house carried its breeding on its ruined face. If challenged to date it, Appleby would have said 1718; if challenged to name the builder, he would have said James Gibbs. But now it spoke either of madness—which, indeed, was what was attributed to its owner—or of penury. Perhaps it spoke of both. Appleby found himself wondering how the false Astarte had risen to a decent coat and skirt when she had presented herself to Gulliver and Heffer on that fateful occasion. For this was Astarte's home. Mysteriously, but finally, Appleby hadn't the slightest doubt of it.

He glanced at Heffer's car. It told him that Heffer

was either a man of unassuming tastes or possessed of
only a very modest private income indeed. He glanced
at the other car, which Parker had supposed to be a
doctor's. There was a brief-case on the back seat—and,
neatly stacked beside it, a sheaf of documents tied with
narrow pink tape. Not a doctor, then. A solicitor. This
discovery was a relief.

Appleby mounted half a dozen steps to the front
door. As he did so, he recalled Sir Gabriel Gulliver's
guess at Astarte Oakes's background: the ponies and
the spaniels in decay, and a garden boy beginning to
feel entitled to a rise in wages. Genteel poverty among
the descendants of a Colonial Governor. Well, that
looked as if it had been a near miss. The poverty was
here, all right. But it didn't seem as if there were a
garden boy. Appleby rang the bell.

Or, rather, he went through the motion of doing this.
But the bell-pull went limp in his hand. It might have
been the limb of an infant corpse—he suddenly and
ghoulishly thought—before *rigor mortis* set in. Then he
remembered a story of a man who had pulled at a
broken bell like this so vigorously that yards of wire
had shot out and strangled him. Veere House, he decided, didn't conduce to a healthy state of mind. He
clenched his fist and knocked vigorously on the door.
After a pause, he knocked again. There was every
reason to suppose that the effect in the interior must
be considerable. But nothing happened. Perhaps he
ought to begin shouting an injunction to open in the
name of the law. But that was more in Parker's line.
He tried the door and found that it wasn't locked. So

he opened it and walked in. Trespass, perhaps. But not house-breaking or burglary.

He was confirmed at once in his impression that here had been a dwelling of some elegance. In front of him was a circular hall of moderate dimensions, rising to a cupola and lantern, and clothed in a plain honey-coloured marble which was relieved by engaged pil-asters in the same stone. Ahead was an archway beyond which a branching staircase rose beneath a second cupola. On either side were open doorways, giving on large rooms.

The hall was quite empty. It could have done with a vigorous wash down, but apart from this it retained the dignity of the day on which it was built. Contrast-ingly, both the rooms leading off it gave an immediate impression of being disgraced. And the reason was obvious. Not only were the carpets and curtains in the last stages of decay. The rooms were crowded—and crowded with junk. It wouldn't all be junk, indeed, if transported to a junk-shop. But it was junk here.

Appleby concentrated on the room on his right. There was a further open door at the other side of it, through which it was possible to see part of another room beyond. This seemed to be crowded in the same way. And neither room was furnished with the slightest attempt at individual character or even specific func-tion. There were beds and there were sideboards. There were desks which looked as if they had come from mas-sive Victorian offices, and there were dressing-tables which looked as if they had come from penurious Vic-torian servants' dormitories. The walls were covered with pictures—oils, water-colours and steel-engravings side by side. There were bags of golf-clubs and bundles of tennis-rackets. There was a vaulting horse and a croquet-box and a stuffed bear and a harmonium. And in the disposition of all these crowded objects there was only one principle to be observed. It was a principle, however, that struck Appleby as a notable one. Nothing was entirely concealed behind anything else.

In the minute which it took Appleby to absorb all this, Veere House was as soundless as the tomb. If the false Astarte were really here, it must surely be in the character of a Sleeping Beauty. In which case, Jimmy Heffer had certainly taken on the rôle of Prince Charming. But whether his plan for arousing the lady was at all moral—whether, indeed, they mightn't both wake up to find themselves in gaol—was a different matter. Anyway, they must now be hunted out. Appleby was about to address himself to this task when he became aware that the deathly stillness of the place had been broken. It had been broken by a light, firm tapping from—he judged—some distant part of the ground floor on which he stood.

The tapping came nearer. You didn't have to remember *Treasure Island* and the blind pirate to be a little unnerved by it. Appleby, who had fought for his life in thieves' kitchens almost as often as Sexton Blake, felt a momentary tingling of the scalp. And then—at the far end of the farther room at which he had been glancing—the occasion of the tapping appeared.

It was an old woman. She came from the shadow of some remoter corridor into a shaft of afternoon sunshine falling through the farthest of a series of windows which extended between Appleby and herself. As she

did so, the sound of her stick—for the tapping did pro-
ceed from a stick—was muted but still irrationally
alarming. She had passed from a tiled floor to a carpeted
one.

It was a quick tapping—so that it suggested itself as
indeed produced by a blind person rather than a lame
one. But this was delusive. The old woman had eyes
that could see. That she was using them was almost
the first impression you had of her. She was advancing
towards Appleby with her head turned steadily to her
left. Her stick was in her right hand. With her left hand
—its index-finger extended—she was making spasmodic
but purposeful movements as she advanced.

She was very old. She was in black. The black was
relieved by a white collar and a white cap. And this,
of course, was what made her uncanny—uncanny as she
advanced through this decorous house, a house of the
kind in which the successors of Sir Christopher Wren
had tactfully refined upon the Dutch taste of William
and Mary. The old woman was like an old woman by
Rembrandt. That was it.

Of course it didn't make sense. Mrs Kipper was not,
presumably, a Kipper. Very probably she had been a
Miss Smith or a Miss Jones. But perhaps she had grown
into the place. . . . Now she had passed into the shadow
between two windows—and now she was in clear faint
sunlight again. She was nearer. And she wasn't—
Appleby saw—a Rembrandt, after all. She was just a
Frans Hals. She hadn't—that was to say—grown out of
the flesh with age. She was an ordinary acquisitive old
woman.

But no—she wasn't quite ordinary, either. She was

behaving in too extraordinary a way. For he could see, now, what that left index-finger was doing. It was ticking things off. It was ticking off all those rubbishing material possessions, no one among which quite concealed any other.

The pathological old miser—for that, of course, was what she was—advanced steadily towards Appleby. She looked at him, and frowned. He ought not to have been there to be counted. She stopped, and spoke sharply.

"Young man," she said, "are you Richardson's clerk?"

It certainly wasn't that she was purblind. A glance from her eyes told you that she saw everything. So Appleby felt rejuvenated. Whether he was a young man was, after all, a relative matter. On the other hand, he certainly wasn't Richardson's clerk. So he had better say so.

"No," he replied. "My name is Appleby, and I have come to call on your niece. You must forgive me for walking in. I seemed to have some difficulty with the bell at the front door."

Mrs Kipper—as she must be presumed to be—ignored this. She had come to a halt for a moment, but now she walked on—crossing her elegant hall and entering the first of the rooms on its farther side. At the same time, she signed to Appleby to accompany her. She gave the impression of being prepared to listen to him, provided this did not distract her from the more important task of checking over her property. This still took place entirely on her left hand. No doubt there was going to be a return journey.

"I asked"—Mrs Kipper said—"because Richardson
is in the house now. I heard his voice as he went upstairs. He has no business here. I have a good mind to
turn him out of the place."

"Isn't Mr Richardson your solicitor?" Appleby asked
this very much at a venture.

"Certainly not. My solicitor is Mr Wiggins of Gray's
Inn. I went up to see him only a few days ago. Richardson is a local man, who did business for my late brother-
in-law, Joseph Kipper. Most mistakenly and unneces-
sarily, Joseph left a sum of money in trust for the education of my niece. Richardson administered it. But that
is all over. The money has been spent and the trust
discharged. The girl may send for him as she pleases.
But he hasn't a penny left to give her, all the same.
Unless out of his own pocket."

"Your niece Astarte?"

Mrs Kipper had now nearly reached the far end of
the room. And she took time off the more serious business of her peregrination to look sharply at Appleby.

"Astarte? Stuff and nonsense! My niece's name is
plain Jane."

"Plain Jane, I am told, is one of the loveliest girls
in England." It was again in an experimental spirit
that Appleby offered this. What it produced from
Mrs Kipper was a cackle of highly disagreeable laughter.

"Lovely? All the more reason why she should marry
Charles Onions. They will cancel each other out, so
far as looks go. Mr Onions is a revoltingly ugly man."

"I see." And indeed Appleby was beginning to see
what might be called the archetypal simplicity of the
situation at Veere House. "Your niece has no wish to

marry this revoltingly ugly man. But she is penniless. And he is the match that you design for her."

"You express it very clearly," Mrs Kipper said. And she walked on. "The announcement," she said presently, "would look well in *The Times*—supposing one were to waste money in that way. Miss J. Kipper and Mr C. Onions. The wedding-photograph, too, would be a joy—supposing one were going to have such a thing."

This time Appleby was silent. Mrs Kipper was not merely disagreeable. She was malignant. And now she had turned and begun moving back the way she had come. If this was a fairy story, Appleby told himself, Mrs Kipper sustained a couple of rôles at once. She was both witch and dragon—and the hoard which the dragon guarded was this dismal accumulation of near-lumber which she had brought together on the ground floor of her house. Probably many of the upper rooms were empty—the mad old creature having concentrated everything down here, the better to keep her eye on it. That would explain the mixture of stuff from bedrooms and drawing-rooms, cloakrooms and libraries. And amid it all—he told himself—there ought to be one supremely interesting object.

"Hasn't your niece ever been prompted to leave home?" Appleby asked. "Isn't she anxious to earn her own living?"

"Her education—thanks to the folly of my brother-in-law—was of the extremely expensive sort that equips a young woman to do nothing. Of course, she might become a shop-girl. And a shop-girl she *will* become, if she doesn't marry Mr Onions."

It was at this moment that Appleby saw the Rembrandt. There was the Old Man—decayed, majestic, translucent, incredible—hanging between an insipid mezzotint and an oblong of chocolate-coated canvas once representing, it might be, a forest scene in the Flemish taste. And for a second Mrs Kipper's eye was resting on it too. But only for a second. The Old Man and his immediate neighbours existed for her, one could see, equally and merely as objects in a compulsive ritual of enumeration.

"I mustn't detain you," Appleby said. It was surprising, he reflected, that this dreadful old person had been willing to suffer him in the way she had. He had better make a further move before her mood altered and she drove him from the house. "If you will be good enough to tell me where I may find Miss Kipper——"

"Upstairs," Mrs Kipper said indifferently. "You can't go wrong."

Without a glance, she tapped her way on into the next room.

CHAPTER FIFTEEN

A MURMUR OF voices guided Appleby when he reached
the first-floor landing. Standing on no ceremony, he
opened a door and walked through it.

He was in the presence—he saw at once—of a council of war. Three people sat round a table. At the head
of it was an elderly man of legal appearance. He must
be Mr Richardson. On his left sat Jimmy Heffer. On
his right sat the girl to whom an ironic fate had given
the beauty of a goddess and the name of Jane Kipper.
Appleby had a second in which to contemplate her with
a certain amount of awe before he was addressed by
Heffer. The young man had sprung to his feet.

"How dare you follow me here!" he said. "How dare
you break into this house!"

"Sit down," Appleby said coldly. "And don't waste
time talking nonsense." He turned to the young woman.
"My name is Appleby. It has probably cropped up in
Mr Heffer's conversation. I see that you have at least
had the good sense to call in legal advice. I understand
this gentleman to be your solicitor, Mr Richardson?"

"Yes." The Botticelli mask was turned gravely on
Appleby. "I sent for him as soon as Jimmy rang up.
Jimmy thought I had killed somebody."

"I really don't think that we can have this." Richardson had stood up and was looking at Appleby with
severity. "Your appearance in this way, Sir John, is
entirely irregular."

"No doubt it is, sir. All the better, perhaps, for your clients."

"Mr Heffer is in no sense my client. Until I entered this room half an hour ago I had never set eyes on him. It is Miss Kipper whose interests I represent. I have stood in a professional relationship to her for many years."

"So I understand. But it appears that she and Mr Heffer have got rather mixed up. They have involved themselves in what might be given the appearance of a criminal conspiracy. I don't doubt that you have learnt that much by this time."

Richardson was silent for a moment. He appeared to be weighing with some care the precise form of words which Appleby had used. Then he relaxed slightly.

"Shall we all sit down?" he said. "We can take it that we know what Sir John is referring to. But I must say at once"—and he turned again to Appleby—"that I can continue this informal discussion only if it is agreed that my client was in no way involved in the death of Sir Gabriel Gulliver. Mr Heffer, it appears, lost his head—conceivably not without your assistance, Sir John—and was disposed to admit what can only be called a morbid and absurd suspicion."

"Mr Heffer, sir, has built up romantic notions of your client, and he has perhaps been inclined to impute to her a degree of ruthlessness which, it is to be hoped, is entirely foreign to her. Although ruthlessness of a sort she certainly has. I don't think that she shot Gulliver this morning. But I'd be glad to hear of a little more positive evidence in the matter than I possess at present."

Richardson nodded.

"As it happens, it exists. Miss Kipper leads a lonely life in this house. She might have difficulty in bringing proof of her whereabouts at one time or another. But, this morning, there were a couple of workmen about the place. Fortunately, she several times conversed with them."

"I accept that." Appleby turned to Heffer. "The nightmare is over, isn't it?" he asked. "You no longer have to think of fighting for your life—and this lady's?"

"Yes. Of course, I knew Jane couldn't have done it, really. But, after the affair last night——"

"No doubt." Appleby interrupted rather brusquely. "And now, we can sort things out a little—factually, if not morally. For I am bound to say, Heffer, that in point of professional trust you have let yourself down badly. Of course, it may be maintained"—and Appleby glanced grimly at the extravagant beauty of Miss Kipper—"that the woman tempted you."

"I can't admit anything of that sort." Richardson struck in sharply. "I cannot admit that Miss Kipper either did, or intended to do, or procure, anything of a criminal nature. There are problems of inheritance in her family—including problems of the rights of owner-ship in various effects in this house—which have never been satisfactorily resolved. One obstacle has been the disposition of her aunt, Mrs Kipper, whom you may have met. It has been my own policy to see what time would do. Mrs Kipper has for long been very eccentric. I happen to know that she visits her own solicitor monthly for the purpose of altering her will. And so forth. It has been in my mind that a long history of such capricious conduct might very usefully be allowed to build itself up—usefully from the point of view of my client, Miss Kipper, should litigation eventually be necessary."

"I understand the force of considerations of that kind, Mr Richardson. And I take it you were not aware that there is a painting of very great value in this house?"

"Certainly I was not aware of it. Nor was Miss Kipper—until a certain recent occasion which we both, I think, have in mind."

"It makes a difference, wouldn't you say? Relatives may disagree about the ownership of a piano, or make off with a dinner service and argue about it afterwards. But when it comes to a proposal to——"

"Quite so." Richardson was looking wary again. "But I must say, Sir John, that I have renewed misgivings about the propriety of this discussion. I think I must advise Miss Kipper—and Mr Heffer, too, for that matter—not to answer questions at this stage."

"Questions?" Appleby shook his head. "My dear sir, I don't intend to ask any. I merely propose—for the sake of clarifying my own mind and yours—to embark on what may be called a brief narrative. I may say that there is only one point in this affair about which I am still seriously in the dark. It will emerge presently, and perhaps I shall get some light on it. May I begin?"

There was a moment's silence. Then—very properly —it was the goddess who spoke.

"Please begin," Jane Kipper said.

"Miss Kipper," Appleby said, "has for long lived

with her aunt in this house in what may be termed a
depressed situation. She has received an expensive, but
not particularly useful, education. But the money has
run out; she is dependent on her miserly relation; her
solicitor can only advise patience. It is all very trying
and vexatious—particularly as Miss Kipper is not
unattractive, and ought therefore, by the law of
nature, to be having a good time."

Appleby paused on this. He knew that these young
people were going to be let off; he knew that he was
himself going to conspire to this end; he didn't see
that he need pull his punches.

"Miss Kipper's expensive education has run to the
history of art. This hasn't, perhaps, put her quite in
the connoisseurs' class—but it has prompted her, one
day, to pause before a certain painting on her aunt's
wall. It is a painting uncommonly like the Rembrandts she has seen when being conducted with her
fellow-pupils round the best galleries. She forms a
plan."

"I just wanted to find out," Jane Kipper said.
"That was how it started, you see."

"Quite so." She was, Appleby reflected, an entirely
commonplace girl. In ten years' time, Jimmy Heffer
would have become aware that his wife was an entirely
commonplace woman. But he was himself an entirely
commonplace man. Only accident had thrust them
into their present uncommon situation. One day there
would be boy Heffers trudging through Eton and
King's, girl Heffers trudging through the best picture
galleries. So be it—Appleby said to himself. Let them
out of this silly jam. Let it all go on.

"Miss Kipper," Appleby said, "forms a design. There is, indeed, one impediment to it. Her aunt keeps an extraordinarily sharp eye upon all her possessions. Mrs Kipper's waking life, in fact, may be described as a sort of sentry-go. Fortunately, however, she does—once a month, or thereabouts—go off the job. Last Friday—a week ago to-day—she goes up to London to see her solicitor, Mr Wiggins of Gray's Inn. That would be right?"

Jane Kipper gave a grave assent.

"So Miss Kipper goes up to London too—with this exciting and problematical painting under her arm. She learns that it is of great value. But she learns this in circumstances of unexpected embarrassment—particularly considering that she has taken the precaution of writing down a false name and address. She learns it in the presence of a young man who is, in fact, known to her. I don't know how this comes about, but the point is not very material."

"My sister and Jane were at the same school," Heffer said. "I recognized her at once, and she recognized me. Since I knew her name, I was able to trace her."

"Heffer," Appleby continued impassively, "lost no time in contacting Miss Kipper. The lady had, as we have noticed, this measure of good looks. And she controlled, even if she did not own, an artistic work of hitherto unsuspected value. I think it conceivable that Miss Kipper somewhat dramatized her situation—and that Mrs Kipper perhaps put in an appearance well-calculated to confirm Heffer in the view that here was a helpless orphan, defrauded of her just rights by an aunt who was little better than an ogre. Be that as it may, it was now Heffer's turn to form a design. He proposed to obtain a replica of the Rembrandt, good enough to pass the daily scrutiny of Mrs Kipper to her dying day, and to sell the original for Miss Kipper's benefit. Mrs Kipper had no interest in the arts, and there was no possibility of the fact of such a transaction coming to her notice. The only serious snag was that Heffer's superior, Sir Gabriel Gulliver, was now aware of the existence of the painting. Heffer and Miss Kipper discussed this. Could he be brought into the plot? Heffer, who knew him very well, did not for a moment believe that he could. Miss Kipper, who considered herself to be a great judge of character, thought otherwise. She believed that she had discerned a certain lack of solidity in Sir Gabriel, which might be played upon. It was thus that, when this morning's fatality took place, Heffer was not free from the appalled sense that Miss Kipper might have tackled Sir Gabriel, discovered her mistake, and killed him to prevent his disclosing the conspiracy. This supposed action of Miss Kipper's was, indeed, a thing very unlikely in the light of last night's events—to which I shall presently come. But Heffer has had a bad morning, all the same."

"It can't be said that you helped," Heffer said.

"I now return"—Appleby continued, unheeding—"to Heffer's design. He knew—or took means to discover—that a man called Trechmann was in a position to have a replica of the Rembrandt made under conditions of secrecy. He entered into negotiations with him. But Mrs Kipper was again a difficulty. The Rembrandt must always be in its accustomed place by day. The only possible arrangement, then, was that Miss Kipper should bring it to Trechmann's shop by night—doing so a sufficient number of times to enable an identical canvas to be painted. And that brings us to six p.m. yesterday evening. At that hour Heffer stepped into Trechmann's shop to confirm the arrangement. As it happened, he stepped straight into another and larger conspiracy—or rather into the fatal consequence of such another conspiracy. He found Trechmann shot dead. It was a great shock to him."

Appleby paused with mild irony on this. Heffer made as if to say something, and then thought better of it.

"And there was an additional awkwardness—as there is apt to be in such amateur attempts at criminal practice. From within seconds of Trechmann's being shot, Heffer was under the observation of the police. He thus had no means of secretly communicating with Miss Kipper and warning her not to turn up with the painting later that night as planned. In the circumstances, he behaved with a certain amount of resource —staging a sort of sit-down strike which enabled him to be on the spot still when Miss Kipper arrived. He gave a warning shout. And Miss Kipper—wearing, I think, the same slacks in which we see her now—bolted, picture and all. This morning seems to have found Heffer somewhat irresolute. He went back to work. He couldn't quite decide what it was safe to do. And so he was overtaken again by events—this time the shooting of Sir Gabriel Gulliver. As soon as he got away from an unpleasant luncheon engagement, however, he beat it for Veere House—followed, naturally, by adequate police observation. So here we are." Appleby paused, and then turned to Richardson. "I believe that I have now sketched the entire course of your client's involvement—and her friend's involvement—in the very grave matters I am investigating."

"Thank you," Richardson said. "The situation, then, is clear. These young people were engaged in a prank, and stumbled upon something very different."

"You may call it a prank if you like—although I'm not at all sure that a judge would agree with you. But my main business is certainly with other characters in the drama."

"Precisely." Richardson appeared eminently satisfied. "Our young friends had this half-baked notion of copying an old painting, and so forth. But it all came to nothing, and we can pass on to more serious matters. If either of them can help you in any way, Sir John, it is a course that I would urge upon them very strongly."

Appleby had taken out his watch and glanced at it.

"I haven't much more time," he said, "for this end of the affair. But there are one or two points I should be glad to have cleared up. The painting of a replica is in itself a perfectly reputable proceeding. But I take it, Heffer, that you felt you had to have it done in a particularly confidential way?"

"Of course I did." Heffer was impatient. "Anybody competent to copy that picture would know what he was copying: an unrecorded Rembrandt of great value. So there must be no tale-telling. That's why I sought out this fellow Trechmann."

"Trechmann was known—at least in a certain limited circle—to be involved in dubious transactions in the field of art-dealing?"

"Yes—in a very limited circle indeed. There was just the beginning of talk about him."

"Had you heard a rumour that Trechmann was in some way connected with definite faking of pictures?"

"Yes—rather obscurely, I had."

Appleby gave a satisfied nod.

"It's a point of some importance. Any talk of that sort would mean that Trechmann's usefulness to certain people who may be called his principals was coming to an end. Did you get the impression that your replica was going to be executed on the premises?"

"That seemed the implication. But I saw no sign of preparation for anything of the sort."

"You wouldn't. Trechmann's shop was connected, by way of the roof, with a studio in which a great deal of enterprising artistic fraud was perpetrated. At least, that is the inference from the evidence that has begun to come in. The occupier of the studio was thick enough with Trechmann to use his drawing pins and index cards in just the way that Trechmann did. And the liquidating of Trechmann was carried out synchronously with a thoroughly efficient emergency evacuation of the studio. In fact it may be said that a very considerable industry was wound up yesterday. But not, perhaps, in a totally negative spirit." Appleby considered for a moment. "Would I be right, Heffer, in supposing that you told this fellow Trechmann more or less your whole story?"

"Yes. I had to. He said he couldn't undertake to

have the copy made without a knowledge of the full circumstances."

"I see. In my opinion—and it's a matter in which I have some experience—you'd never make other than rather a naïve crook. Good afternoon."

And Appleby didn't wait to see the young man flush. He had got to his feet, bowed to Richardson and the astounding Miss Kipper, and walked out of the room. Veere House and its denizens were no longer of much interest to him. It was Rose Cottage, Winterbourne Crucis, that he was beginning to wonder about.

CHAPTER SIXTEEN

The light was fading as Appleby drove back through Woodford. He had parted from both Parker and his own driver, and was at the wheel of the big police car himself. He had an instinct for solitude at this stage of an affair. And it is something you get—after a fashion—when driving a car into London against rush-hour traffic. He decided to go straight home. It was too early for Judith to be back—too early by a good bit. All the same, he'd get straight back to Westminster.

It seemed a long time ago that this had been the Manallace mystery. But it was only yesterday that he had been listening, idly enough, first to Charles Gribble's innocent delight and then to Charles Gribble's comical dismay. It had been a few hours after that, again, that Gabriel Gulliver had got talking, and that the mighty name of Rembrandt had in consequence come up over the horizon. In history—criminal history —it would be as the Rembrandt mystery that this would go down. He wondered what would happen to Mrs Kipper's Old Man. Perhaps Richardson, who was a shrewd chap, would establish that it was really Miss Kipper's Old Man. In which case it would probably end by making Jimmy Heffer's fortune after all. One wouldn't be able to call that a very moral conclusion to the affair. Not that it would matter very much in the world in which the Old Man lived. In that world the Old Man was lodged timelessly.

When old age shall this generation waste,
   Thou shalt remain——

Appleby braked smoothly. The London Hospital again. And another ambulance.

Six o'clock came tumbling down from Big Ben as he turned out of Whitehall. Five minutes later he was on the pavement before his own front door. As he felt for his latch-key a car drew up behind him. He glanced at the man getting out of it. He was Jimmy Heffer.

"That sort of trailing is easier than I thought." Heffer jerked out the words nervously as he came up. "Do you mind, sir? Can I have just another word with you?"

Appleby nodded silently. He didn't want this. But he could see that something had cracked in Heffer. The young man had been realizing things. Appleby opened the door, switched on a light, and led the way to his study.

"Yes?" he said, without sitting down.

"I wanted to say this: that it did seem to me, on the facts, to be justly and honestly Jane's. The damned picture, I mean."

"Jane, did you say? Quite a lot seems to have been happening at high speed in this bad business."

"Yes, I know. But she did turn out to like me, you see. Just as I liked her."

"And so you set out on more justice and honesty together." Appleby looked at the young man steadily. "Heffer, there's only one thing it occurs to me to say. Queer things can happen to a man's judgement in the face of beauty like that. I've never seen such a girl.

And you'd never seen such a girl. As for the girl herself, I don't see her as carrying much responsibility. For her, quite genuinely, the picture was just a piece of disputed family property, no doubt. But for you, you know, it was something that came along in the course of your job. And one's job comes first."

"Don't think I don't understand that. I'll live with it, all right. But, you see, there's another thing."

"Yes?" Appleby waited. He knew what was coming.

"Gulliver. I must know about that, please. Am I responsible?"

"Yes and no. If you hadn't started what you did, your chief would be alive now. But what has happened isn't anything you could possibly have conceived of as likely to flow from what you did. That's all I can say. And now——"

A telephone bell rang sharply in the room. Appleby turned and picked up the receiver. He listened, and his expression changed instantly. He turned, still listening, and pointed through the open door of the room. There was a second instrument on a table in the hall. And Heffer understood at once. He was out of the room in a flash, and listening to what followed.

"Yes," Appleby said. "Sir John Appleby speaking."

"Splendid," a man's voice said. "I wonder if you know who I am?"

"Certainly I do. Carl Bendixson."

"Excellent. You're good at guessing. In fact, I think you've been guessing a good deal?"

"You're right. I have."

"For instance, that I was under that newspaper when Gribble was gassing away at the club?"

"Of course." Appleby had turned pale, but his voice was steady. "And that you knew Trechmann would give the show away if put in a really tight spot. And that you were good enough to dine with my wife and myself immediately after killing the man. And that you left early for the purpose of cleaning up the studio in which your wife perpetrated her fakes."

"Splendid again. I say, isn't this a queer conversation?"

"I see no need to characterize its quality. Say what you have to say."

"All in good time. Have you anybody listening in on this, by the way? If so, I hope he's thoroughly reliable."

"I have, and he is. I'd describe him as somebody I'm inclined to trust. Continue."

There was a moment's pause. It was as if Carl Bendixson's confidence was momentarily shaken.

"It was odd, Appleby, that you should pick on me to ask about Van Gogh's eye. That told me you were on the trail, all right. And I suppose you're clear about that ass Gulliver?"

"I am. You realized that the picture-faking racket was packing up on you. You had heard about the Rembrandt from Trechmann. You believed that, once they had committed themselves to a criminal act, it could be extorted from Heffer and Miss Kipper by threats. And that Gulliver was the only other person who knew about it. You decided to make a bid for such an enormous prize. Your wife called on Gulliver, confident that she could make him an accomplice. Gulliver had passed on to Lord Mountmerton some nonsense you'd fed him about a niece of Van Gogh's, and your wife mistook casualness for lack of scruple. As it happened, Gulliver was a thoroughly honourable man. Quite a lot of men are. So she had to cover her tracks by shooting him. It is a family habit you appear to have formed."

"Very true, Appleby. It is a thing that comes more easily with practice. Reflect on that."

There was again a moment's pause. This time, it was on Appleby's part. When he did speak, it was as calmly as before.

"Have you anything more to say, Bendixson? It's rather risky, you know, prolonging a telephone call of this sort. The police have their resources in these matters."

"No doubt. And they are really quite fast workers, I admit. Sending your wife jaunting off to Winterbourne Crucis was quite a bit of hustling, was it not? She happened to mention where she was going to a friend of mine."

"Miss Wildsmith?" Appleby had gone quite tense.

"Yes—our delightful Mary. Mary rang me up at once. In a sense, I had to admit that the game was up. We were very careful about that studio in Bloomsbury. You wouldn't have connected us with it at all easily. But we were careless about the fascinating Mme de la Gallette's cottage, I admit. It's rented in my name. I am a shade rash at times. And injudiciously frolicsome. All that Manallace nonsense, for example. Fun —but injudicious. Mary, by the way, has departed. She will be in France by now, and your chances of tracing her are negligible. Gretta and I, on the other hand, require a little time. If we are to do things comfortably, that is to say—and depart with such material goods as we are minded to depart with. Hence this call."

"Go on."

"All this is under your hat. That's your habit, as your wife was good enough to inform us. None of your people are at present effectively in the picture. And you will freeze the whole affair, please, for forty-eight hours from this moment. If, that is to say, you want your wife returned to you. Good-bye."

It was over. Heffer was back in the room.

"It can't be true!" he said. "Such things just——"

"One thing does lead to another, Heffer. And, meantime, one's job remains one's job." Appleby was quite still for a moment. He was looking at Heffer unseeingly when his eyes suddenly lit up. He whirled round to a bookcase and seized a book. It was an atlas.

"But they simply couldn't——"

"Don't waste time. Take my car to the corner of the street and fill up with petrol. Then come back." Appleby picked up the telephone again. "The fellow's mad. What does he think of me? I've got to call the Yard. And the Admiralty. Can you use a revolver?"

"Yes."

"I'm going on rather a risky trip. Will you come with me?"

There was a second's pause. It was because Heffer wasn't quite sure of his voice.

"Anywhere," he said, a little huskily.

CHAPTER SEVENTEEN

Silence observed ... forty-eight hours ...
we're not on the telly yet.

But we well might be, Appleby thought, as the
Aston Martin roared through the late evening. The
very air it was displacing was filled, he knew, with
short-wave signals reaching to every corner of the
country and beyond. But he was his own best hope.

For forty racing miles Heffer hadn't dared to speak.
But now he did.

"Is this a D.B.4?" he asked—and was instantly
aware of the horrible fatuity of such a question.

But Appleby answered quietly.

"Yes—and just run in. But one wants an Autobahn
if it's really to show its paces."

Heffer found the self-control of this steadying.

"You have a clue, sir?"

"I think so. I think Judith isn't the only one to
have given something away. The Bendixson woman
... at that accursed dinner-party ... talking her
nauseous nonsense about antiques ... not that we
don't do it ourselves——" Appleby was speaking spas-
modically as he swung the wheel. "Something about
picking up a small treasure in a junk shop on the
south coast. A place where they keep their yacht ...
glorified motor-boat of some sort, I don't doubt. ...
And ocean-going, wouldn't you say? Place called
Bryne Bay, not far from Lymington. . . . Been through

it once . . . still a confoundedly long way off." Appleby thrust down the accelerator another fraction. "But not so far from their precious Rose Cottage in the New Forest."

"But why that telephone-call, at all? Why that forty-eight hours? Why didn't they just *go*?"

"Because I'd have been on top of them in twelve hours . . . on top of them in six. Do you think I'd have gone to sleep if Judith hadn't turned up? Do you think my brain would have stopped working?" For the first and only time that night, Appleby's voice rose a pitch. "I'd have had all France alerted by dawn. And the sea swept beyond Ushant." Appleby was silent for a moment. He took a corner with care. "In half an hour we'll have a moon," he said quietly.

"How did that Mary Wildsmith come in? She isn't a painter. And do you think she has really got clean away?"

"She could put on an act, either in French or English, as the mistress, daughter, grandchild or whatever of one eminent painter or another—and as one happily still in possession of some priceless masterpiece. You can control great companies, it seems, and yet be completely gullible when you think you have a chance of getting ahead of other collectors. I formed the impression that she is a highly intelligent woman— which, no doubt, helps. And I think it unlikely that she will ever be traced. She probably possesses the necessary papers, and can fade into a French identity somewhere without the slightest difficulty. A pity—but I don't feel vindictive about her. . . . The acceleration is good." Appleby had turned into a straight stretch, and Heffer felt the car hit him in the back. "There's a revolver in the glove-box. You'd better investigate it."

After a rainy day the moon had come up in a clear sky. It was silvering the Channel when they caught a first glimpse of it. As they roared through the single silent street of Bryne Harbour it glinted on a hanging sign that said "Antiques".

"Where they got their damned 'spones with knopis'," Appleby said. "But it doesn't follow——"

"Look!"

Heffer was leaning forward, breathless. Straight ahead of them, its landward end concealed by a group of sheds, a low pier ran on a gentle curve far out to sea. A few small craft were moored in its lee; two or three others were at anchor in the bay. But it was something else which had drawn an excited shout from Heffer. A large car had been driven to the point of the pier, and a motor-boat lay just beneath it. There were moving lights. And it was just possible to see moving figures.

"Yes," Appleby said. "Yes—it can be nothing else. Not at this time. It's them. And we can run straight up behind them. Have that gun ready." He swung round the sheds, and a second later was braking hard. There was a crash, and they were both thrown forward in their seats. A van had been drawn up dead across the entrance to the pier. They had gone straight into it.

Appleby was out and running. But Heffer was before him. They scrambled over the van and tore down the pier. The crash had echoed through the night. There was a warning shout from ahead. The motor-boat rocked violently. Its engine spluttered, roared into life, spluttered and died again. Heffer was still ahead—and so far ahead that Appleby wondered whether he himself had been hurt without knowing it and was merely stumbling forward. And then he remembered. The four hundred metres. Jimmy Heffer was a man who, when on form, would cover that distance rather notably. Say in forty-eight seconds flat.

But now the engine was roaring again. Appleby saw the nose of the motor-boat move and turn. Then clear water between its stern and the pier. Heffer was still running. Now he had taken a flying leap—a leap you could hardly believe in. The motor-boat veered wildly; there were shouts, a shot, and then it was moving with gathering momentum on a straight course. But now there was another sound—the answering roar of a second engine from somewhere beyond the bay. A plume of spray appeared, a low grey craft, a trail of foam. It was a Coast-Guard cutter.

What followed, happened with horrifying swiftness. The two hurtling craft were close together. There was another shot from the motor-boat, another shout—and suddenly it had turned sharply and turned again, completely out of control. The cutter, taking evasive action too late, caught it bow-on. As the concussion echoed across the bay, and as the cutter swung in a wide arc to return to the scene of the collision, the motor-boat parted in two, like a toy, and sank.

A second later, Appleby was swimming.

The bodies of Carl and Gretta Bendixson had both

been recovered. They lay on the pier. Somebody had found a tarpaulin to cover them with. They might have been merchandise—a small quantity of ship's stores, waiting to be loaded.

Judith Appleby sat on a bollard. She was chafing her ankles.

"You see, they tied me up," she said. "Fair enough, after all the kicking I did. But to be treated not as a person at all—to be treated as a physical object—by people who ate their last dinner off you: it's a shock." She smiled rather wanly at her husband. "Wasn't I an ass—giving myself away to Mary Wildsmith like that? Giving you the hell of a drive—and a wetting."

Appleby felt for cigarettes—and then remembered that, in a man who has had the hell of a wetting, this is a useless gesture. He couldn't trust himself to speak.

"That young man—he'll be all right?"

"Heffer? Yes, he'll be all right. He's in the ambulance now. A bullet got him in the shoulder."

"Bendixson knocked him out, and he came up again. Gretta shot him and he came up again. It was during the second scrap that the tiller went. Lucky about the cutter. You must have got organized pretty fast, John. As I'd expect."

Appleby put out a hand.

"Get up," he said. "We go home now."